Kazu Jones

AND THE
COMIC BOOK CRIMINAL

Kazu Jones

AND THE
COMIC BOOK CRIMINAL

by SHAUNA HOLYOAK

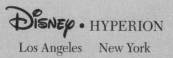

DISNEY • HYPERION
Los Angeles   New York

First Edition, April 2020
10 9 8 7 6 5 4 3 2 1
FAC-020093-20066

Printed in the United States of America

This book is set in New Caldonia LT STD / Adobe; Apsirin ITC Std /
International; Arian LT / Monotype
Designed by Jamie Alloy

Library of Congress Cataloging-in-Publication Data on file
ISBN 978-1-368-02267-5

Reinforced binding

Visit www.DisneyBooks.com

To my nerdy family, who understands that everyone needs room for their weird

CHAPTER ONE

"I'm activating Grand Hacker's laser eyes to incinerate the Mutilator." March scrunched his face as he moved his plastic miniature to the back corner of the gaming mat.

I let out a huff. The Mutilator had me pinned in a corner of the nuclear junkyard, my back against an old reactor. March's move could destroy me.

Owen, March's uncle and our Game Master, tsked. "Doing so puts Golden Specter in danger. She may not survive the blast, especially if the reactor contains any radioactivity."

Even in danger, I smiled to hear Owen say my character name aloud: Golden Specter. If only I could get kids at school to call me that.

1

As if he could read my mind, March said, "Kazu, the Golden Specter? More like Golden Cockroach. She can survive anything, even a radioactive explosion." He rolled the dice and scoffed. "What?! Three? No way!"

"Grand Hacker singes the Mutilator's eyebrows," Owen said, and even I could tell he was trying not to chuckle. Owen's dark curls were pulled from his pale face into a funky ponytail at the top of his head. He looked exactly how I thought March would look in twenty years. "Your blast distracts the Mutilator, and he turns his attention from the Golden Specter to your character." Owen went back to studying his notes, which were splayed over the front page of today's newspaper.

CindeeRae rubbed her hands together as March pushed the dice toward her. At first, I had been surprised that she liked playing Defender, March's favorite role-playing game, nearly as much as March did. But I should have expected the theater nerd, who was also the newest member of our detective team, to enjoy a game where you got to act like a superhero on a special mission.

For the past month the team had been playing Defender on Wednesday afternoons at the Super Pickle: Comics and More. Owen owned the place, which was just outside our neighborhood, and I knew March spent most of his allowance here. He had hundreds of comics stored in narrow cardboard drawers that slid under his bed. On Tuesday nights he came here to play with his dad in a local tournament for a geeky card game called Sorcery. Owen had once told March he could start working at the Super Pickle when he turned fourteen, and ever since then March had become almost as devoted to Owen's business as Owen himself.

CindeeRae twirled her caped miniature on the board like it was doing pirouettes. She had painted the figurine to look just like her, with flaming red hair and green pinpoint eyes. "The Lavish Director wants to know if it's possible to use her telekinetic powers to launch the reactor onto the Mutilator's head."

Owen's eyes glazed over as he stared at the newspaper, so I answered for him. "Golden Specter may have escaped the Mutilator's grasp, but she's still right there. Close enough that the reactor might crush her, too." To emphasize my point, I reached across the mat and made my miniature jump up and down next to the villain. "This is a cooperative game, guys. We should be looking out for one another."

"Oh, I see," March said, his expression fake-serious. "Like when you time-warped me out of the game for five turns so I could break into the Mutilator's lair and blow up his arsenal?"

"It would've worked if you had rolled higher." I crossed my arms and leaned back in my chair, which bumped into CindeeRae's. Owen's store was cramped with boxes of comics sitting on rectangular tables that lined the walls, with even more boxes stored underneath. There was hardly enough room to walk around. The square card table had been squeezed into the center of the store, with most of the chair backs touching.

CindeeRae picked up her miniature and waved it around like she was trying to hypnotize us. "Lavish Director exercises her powers of compulsion to calm her teammates so they get along."

Owen finally snapped to attention and stood, the newspaper clenched in his fist and his game notes fluttering to the floor. "I think this is a good stopping point."

"What?" we all said in a chorus.

"But the Mutilator is right there." March pointed at the board like we couldn't all see the dark, hulking miniature.

"Sorry, guys." Owen set down the newspaper and opened up the box so he could pack up the game. "This whole vandalism thing has got me a little distracted."

The paper's headline read "Vandal Hits Third Comic Book Store," above a report on the graffiti that now plastered the front of Comic Warehouse in Lincoln Park. I only knew because I had read the article after my newspaper route that morning; all good detectives kept up with current events.

"They wouldn't dare vandalize the Super Pickle." March gently cupped the miniatures in his palm before setting them in the box. CindeeRae climbed under the table to gather Owen's notecards.

"Maybe," Owen said. "It's just, this business hardly makes any money as it is. They say the hits might be gang-related, and if the Super Pickle became a target, that kind of publicity would end me." He dropped the mat into the box and closed it.

March's face darkened, alarm radiating from him like heat.

"Don't worry," I said, more to March than Owen. "It won't happen. The Super Pickle will be fine."

Even so, I couldn't stop thinking about the article's closing line, a conclusion that had probably worked Owen into an anxious frenzy: The vandal appeared intent on striking again.

• • •

I kicked my shoes off in the entryway to our house, Genki's tail thwapping against the door as he ran to greet me. CindeeRae and I had spent the rest of the afternoon at March's after our game got cut short at the Super Pickle. I came home just in time for dinner; no sooner and no later.

"Is that you, Kazu?" my grandma called from the kitchen, her voice stiff. Baa-chan had come to visit after Mom got sick last week, and I was still adjusting.

The smell of something spicy drifted toward me, and for the hundredth time I wished Mom felt good enough to make one of my favorites. Baa-chan *knew* I didn't like spicy food.

"Do you need help?" I stopped at the end of the counter.

Baa-chan stood at the oven, stirring a big pot on the stovetop. She was wrapped in one of Mom's fancy aprons with a thick ruffle at the bottom, and somehow it made her look smaller. Even still, I was certain she could command an army.

Unsure what to do with my hands, I clasped them in front of me. Genki stood at my feet, watching my face like I was sending a coded message.

"Sit," Baa-chan said as she spooned something into bowls. I slid into a bar chair just as Genki sat back on his haunches.

Baa-chan turned to see us both, perfectly obedient. "Not you," she scolded me. *"Him."*

Genki's tail beat the floor, as if he'd just earned a T-R-E-A-T.

"Help me bring dinner to the table, please." She held out a bowl, split in half with rice on one side and what looked like stew on the other.

Without thinking, I wrinkled my nose.

"You haven't even tried it," she said, her eyebrows high and disapproving.

I stood and took the bowl, trying to shake the twisted expression from my face. "It looks good," I lied. "What is it?"

"Curry rice."

As I followed her into the dining room, I watched the curry juice seep into the white rice, spreading slow and heavy like lava. Genki stayed behind, his tail still drumming the kitchen floor. Dad's footfalls thundered on the stairs, and his hello bellowed through the house.

"Good evening," Baa-chan replied.

After Mom had gone to the doctor last week, Baa-chan had flown into town from Nagano, Japan, where she and my grandpa Jii-chan lived. All week long, Mom had been pale and shaky, sleeping for hours at a time. When I asked what was wrong, Dad had mumbled something about her needing rest. "It's nothing for you to worry about, Bug," he had said, ruffling my hair. "And sometimes even moms need their mothers to take care of them."

So while Mom recovered from her mystery illness, Baa-chan was here to parent us all, which was a lot like having a grouchy substitute teacher take over and give you more math homework than your real teacher ever would have required.

I sat at my place and fiddled with my soup spoon as Dad peeked into the dining room. From my spot at the table I could see that Genki had given up on getting a treat, dropping to a ball beneath the kitchen counter, his butt wedged beneath a chair.

"Howdy, Bug!" Dad eyed me for a second before noticing Genki. "You hungry, boy?"

Genki stood, nearly knocking over the chair and starting a whirlwind with his tail.

"That dog is spoiled," Baa-chan snapped as she walked back into the kitchen. I rolled my eyes at Dad to let him know what I thought of that.

Dad winked before walking through the kitchen to the laundry room, where we kept the dog food. I could hear the clicking of Genki's nails on the kitchen tile, marching in place as he waited for Dad to dish out his dinner. The clicking intensified, like he was performing the finale of a doggie tap dance. "Okaa-san," Dad shouted; he called Baa-chan *mother* in Japanese because he said it was respectful. "Where's Genki's food?"

"In the garage," Baa-chan said from the kitchen. "Dogs shouldn't eat in the house."

I caught my tongue between my teeth, holding it tight until the pinch made my eyes sting. Baa-chan insisted we follow her rules so she could lessen Mom's load. It wasn't working. In just one week, Baa-chan had become the heavy-browed boss of the house. But talking back to Baa-chan upset Mom, and I didn't want to spend what little time I had with her apologizing for being rude to my elders. The garage door opened and closed, and I told myself Genki didn't care *where* he ate as long as someone fed him.

Dad came back into the dining room, having left Genki in the garage with his dinner. I tapped my spoon on the curry bowl as Baa-chan returned, carrying a pitcher full of mugicha. She looked pointedly at me until I stopped the tapping, then sat at the table and shook her napkin onto her lap.

"Is Mom coming down?" I asked, drilling Dad with my eyes.

Baa-chan answered for him. "She's resting. I'll bring her dinner up when we've finished."

Dad looked at the table instead of me.

Baa-chan's face suddenly relaxed. "Please eat," she said.

"Itadakimasu," Dad said—which meant "I humbly partake" in Japanese—and scooped up a heaping spoonful. Then he stopped to ask, "What did *you* do today, Kazu?"

"We played Defender at the Super Pickle." I held my spoon at my lips, tempted to stick my tongue out to test the curry. "But we didn't play for very long because Owen is freaked out about the vandal hitting comic book stores."

"What are we talking about?" Baa-chan leaned over the table as Dad shoveled another bite into his mouth.

"Some guy is spray-painting graffiti all over comic book stores," I explained. "And March's uncle was already thinking about closing the Super Pickle since it doesn't make very much money. He might finally give up if the vandal hits his store."

"Oh!" Baa-chan said before Dad could pipe in. "I saw that story in the newspaper this morning. It looks like the vandal is a street artist."

"A what?" I finally took the bite of curry and moved it around in my mouth. My eyebrows shot up in surprise. It tasted like a cozy spot in front of the fire, not too spicy but warm enough to tingle my tongue.

"Street artists are serious about their craft," she said. "And they use art to share a message. That doesn't mean it would be right to vandalize your Super Pickle, it just means they have a reason for doing it that's important to them."

I squinted at Baa-chan, surprised she knew so much about graffiti. "Don't tell March that."

"March *is* serious about his comic book stores," Dad agreed, his mouth half-full. "Especially the Super Pickle."

I nodded, tired already of sharing this discussion with Baa-chan, who was making it feel more like a school lecture than dinner conversation.

"What do you think of the curry?" she asked.

I slowly chewed the bite I had just taken, waiting a few seconds before swallowing. "It's okay," I said. My mouth suddenly tasted sour from the fib I had just told.

"Hurry and finish eating." Baa-chan finally picked up her spoon and dug through the rice and curry for a balanced bite. "You still have chores to finish before bedtime."

I wrinkled my nose again, only this time on purpose. No one likes a grouchy substitute.

CHAPTER TWO

March pulled out yesterday's newspaper after we finished lunch on Thursday, being sure to clean the table with a napkin before spreading out the article and smoothing it with gentle fingers. CindeeRae and I exchanged glances. I was pretty sure March planned to pitch a new case focusing on the vandal he and Owen were worried about.

He brushed down his shirt like it was a power suit. Actually, the crisp T-shirt he wore had Colonel Nightmare on the front, a mutant scientist from a comic whose face was covered in scars that looked like melted cheese.

CindeeRae had pushed her chair away from the table, helping her maintain a safe distance from the newspaper.

Ever since we had busted the Denver Dognapping Ring, she had been wary of taking on another dangerous case.

But I was ready for a new challenge; it had been *months* since we had done any detecting. I shifted in my seat, waiting for March to speak, and when he didn't, I let out a big huff. "Well?"

After one last deep breath, he finally began. "As you know, a vandal has struck three comic book stores in the Denver area." March sounded like a newscaster; I imagined him practicing the speech early this morning after I had delivered his family's newspaper. Before the dognapper case, when our detective team was just two members big, I would pick our cases and nag March into helping me solve them. Now that we were a team of three, everyone had to agree on which cases we took on. "According to this article, they expect him to strike again, and the Super Pickle is a potential target."

March paused dramatically until a clanging from the kitchen broke the mood.

"Hurry up, March," CindeeRae said, using her theater voice. "What are you proposing?"

He picked up the paper and held out the front page so we could see. "As you know, the last hit was at Comic Warehouse."

The *Denver Chronicle* had reported on each of the three hits in the article. The first was at Mile High Comics, where a gigantic toilet bowl was practically buried by a mound of comics. In the second hit, the entire storefront of Comic Relief was covered with a picture of a landfill stacked to the clouds with comic books.

Despite herself, CindeeRae leaned forward to get a better look at the third hit, and together we peered at the picture. Comic Warehouse was a blocky brick building with no windows. The entire storefront was covered in a mural of a ginormous superhero guzzling a stack of comic books. It was pretty amazing—you know, if it wasn't a crime.

March continued, "Owen knows the owner and offered to help him paint over the graffiti tomorrow. If we help, we could also gather clues. You know. For our new case: tracking down the comic-hating vandal."

CindeeRae's eyebrows shot up. "Wait a minute. It's not a *new* case until we vote." Her braids knocked against her shoulders as she shook her head. "Are we sure that hunting down a graffiti artist—"

"Vandal." March's head snapped up when he said it.

"*Van-dal.*" CindeeRae said each syllable like it was its own word. "Isn't dangerous? I mean, we just barely got out of trouble for the last case we solved." I could see her point. We had all been grounded for a few weeks after we busted the dognapping ring wide open with our detecting brilliance. But our parents and the police thought it was reckless and all kinds of illegal. We had to do community service for twenty hours each at

14

the Denver Police Department's K-9 unit and promise Detective Hawthorne we would never meddle in an open investigation again.

But that didn't mean we couldn't search for clues or gather evidence. I knew because I had asked. Detective Hawthorne had clarified that we could research crimes, but we couldn't break any laws or interfere with police work; he then made us each write a paper detailing everything we had done on the dognapper case that was illegal or obstructive. The team hadn't been happy about that assignment.

March's lips tightened into a thin, straight line, and his eyebrows huddled up. "Investigating a vandal isn't dangerous. Besides, it's important to Owen and the other comic book stores."

I was mostly on his side, even though I wasn't as interested in bringing the vandal to justice as much as I wanted something to distract me from Mom's strange illness and Baa-chan's iron house rule. Plus, following a street artist would be cool. "But do we have enough clues to launch an investigation?" I met his eyes, willing him to give us more to go on.

He finally sat down, relaxing his shoulders as he slumped in his seat. "That's why we need to visit the crime scene."

Calling Comic Warehouse a crime scene definitely made the case more appealing to me. Not so much for

CindeeRae, whose forehead wrinkled, a crease settling between her eyebrows.

The bell rang, followed by a momentary silence before kids barreled down the hallway outside the cafeteria, the chatter quickly becoming a thunderous pounding of feet and echoing conversations. March sighed. "We'll pick this up later," he said. He had just begun gathering his things when Madeleine Brown slithered through the door and stopped at our table, her fist falling like a paperweight onto the newspaper.

"What's going on?" she asked. Tall, Korean, athletic, and bossy most of the time, Madeleine had joined our team to catch the dognappers last fall, hoping to free her own dog, Lenny. After we had cracked the case, she had gone back to her life as a fifth-grade soccer star, although rumor had it that she had just quit the team. No one knew why.

Madeleine seemed to have become a reformed bully after we closed the case. She wasn't super friendly, but she wasn't super mean either—she mostly ignored us, which is the best you could hope for with Madeleine Brown. I decided she had gifted us the power of invisibility, and I wasn't keen on any take-back-sies.

"What do you want, Madeleine?" I asked, my voice pounding each syllable of her name.

Madeleine looked at the paper, a smile tugging at her lips. "Just wondering if you snoops were trying to crack this case, too." She smoothed down her shirt, a bright orange jersey with a hedgehog on the front. "You know what they say about strength in numbers."

I stood to toss my lunch sack into the garbage and then faced Madeleine across the table. "You want to join the team again?"

Madeleine shrugged. "Why not?"

"Because you were mean," CindeeRae interrupted. "And bossy."

March cocked his head as he watched CindeeRae and Madeleine face off, like they were a strange exhibit at the zoo. The silence swelled around us.

"I know I wasn't the nicest person, but being on your team made me better," Madeleine said quietly. "Right?" She looked at each of us, waiting for a response.

"I mean, yeah," I said. "But how do we know you won't change back?"

She searched the room as if she had hidden a cheat sheet somewhere. "I stopped those dog fighters from getting March."

Madeleine had once saved March from the bad guys, turning back for him after he'd tripped in the abandoned amusement park where we were being chased. It was a moment that had surprised us all, maybe even Madeleine herself.

When we didn't respond, she sighed. "Please?"

It was obvious Madeleine wanted to help, and the

nice thing to do would be invite her back. But March, CindeeRae, and I were the team now, and I couldn't make a decision like that without them. Besides, I wasn't even sure *I* wanted her around.

When we didn't answer, Madeleine's expression hardened into a glare, and she mumbled under her breath, "You guys are jerks. I thought we were friends." She spun around and stomped out of the cafeteria without looking back.

My gaze followed her and remained fixed even after she had disappeared down the hallway. "She's not wrong."

"Really?" CindeeRae's lips puckered. "You want her to help us solve this case?"

"She *was* a lot of help busting the dognappers. Plus, she got nicer."

"Wait." March's voice came out squeaky. "Does that mean we're taking on this case?"

CindeeRae rolled her eyes, realizing she'd accidentally called March's recent pitch a *case.* "Fine," she said. "Let's do it."

March looked at me, excitement making his smile all twitchy. "Kazu?"

I nodded. My chest fluttered at the idea of opening a new investigation, and I was so distracted by the feeling, I nearly jumped out of my skin when the second bell rang.

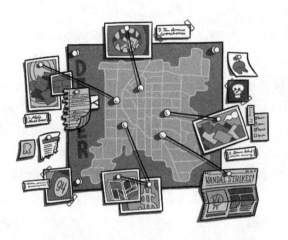

CHAPTER THREE

I snuck into the house without saying a word and climbed the stairs to Mom's room before Baa-chan caught me. The door creaked as I pushed it open. I stepped inside, letting my eyes adjust to the darkness, and Genki followed me. The blackout curtains were drawn, and the room smelled like damp towels and dirty laundry; I scrunched my nose as I walked closer to the bed.

"Mom?" She was lying under a heap of blankets, her head hidden. When she didn't answer, I croaked, "Moooooom?"

"Mmmmm?" she moaned.

I dropped my backpack and climbed onto Dad's side

of the bed, careful not to jostle the mattress. "How are you feeling?"

Genki jumped up behind me and began digging around the foot of the bed to make a blanket nest. Even though we both knew this bed was strictly off-limits, Mom didn't notice, and I let him stay.

"Tired." She sounded like she was sleep-talking. And then she mumbled, so softly I wasn't sure I heard her right, "And sad."

Sad? Why was Mom sad? Had she been sad this whole time, or just today?

I thought back to when she had stopped coming downstairs after the doctor's appointment, a little over a week ago—when Baa-chan came. Before that Mom had been perfectly healthy, going for a jog every day after sending me off to school and then working at the museum. But now her usually sleek and shiny hair lay matted and dull. Her brown eyes were surrounded by dark circles and her skin was pale. How could things change so quickly?

"We should go for a walk." Maybe she'd feel better if she got up and felt the sun on her face. All the snow had melted while she'd been up here, and the change in weather might turn everything around.

She closed her eyes again and said, "I'm not feeling up to it, Kazu." Her hand peeked from under the sheets and covered mine. It was still soft and warm. "I'm sorry."

I nodded and smiled even though my eyes stung. "Can I just lie here with you for a while?"

"Of course, sweetie." She closed her eyes and released a deep sigh. "Tell me about your day."

I talked about playing Defender at the Super Pickle yesterday, and how March and Owen were worried about the vandal hitting his store next. She smiled when I imitated March's stiff presentation at lunch, pleading with CindeeRae and me to take on the case. I told her that Madeleine wanted in, but CindeeRae and I weren't sure about that.

"No meddling in police work." Her froggy voice still had that annoying mom pitch, but this time the familiar tone echoed through my whole body, making all the heavy places feel suddenly light. Maybe Mom was getting better already.

"We won't," I said quickly. "I promise."

I reached my foot out to scratch Genki's belly and he rolled over, pushing his chest toward me. "Let's watch a movie," I said, but Mom had already fallen asleep.

Mom was sick or sad or something, and no one was telling me why. My heart swelled like a puffer fish, prickling in my chest as I imagined what might be wrong. What if, unlike what Dad had said, this *was* something to worry about? Maybe Mom wouldn't get better, but worse, and he was just too afraid to break it to me.

A little detecting could help me figure it out for

myself. I crawled under the comforter and snuggled as close to her as I could without waking her up. I had never had two open cases at the same time, but this might be the most important investigation of my life.

• • •

After school the next day, March, CindeeRae, and I grabbed our bikes and headed to Comic Warehouse. CindeeRae had play rehearsal that night—she was Ladybug in the local production of *James and the Giant Peach*—so we needed to hurry if we were going to help with cleanup *and* find the clues we needed for our investigation. As we waited to cross an intersection just three blocks from the school, CindeeRae squawked at something behind us.

We all turned to see Madeleine skid to a stop on her bike, her front tire nearly colliding with CindeeRae.

Madeleine unfastened her helmet and shook out her hair. It sprung from her head frizzy and wild. "Look," she said, "I understand why you don't want me on the team. So I'm here to ask for a trial period."

CindeeRae folded her arms tightly across her chest.

"Let me work with you on this case." Madeleine studied our faces, biting at her thumbnail. "If you don't like working with me, you can kick me off the team. Anytime. No questions asked."

"Did you follow us here?" CindeeRae asked, and when Madeleine nodded, she muttered, "Stalker."

"Is that a no?" I asked CindeeRae.

"An observation," she answered.

"Before you decide," Madeleine cut in, ignoring CindeeRae, "I know a lot about comics. Next to soccer, it's my thing. So I really could help."

"Not that we need it," March said, and then shrugged, "but it's okay with me." After Madeleine had rescued him at Magic Planet, he had developed a soft spot for her.

"I vote yes," I said, mostly because if Madeleine cared enough to follow us here, she must be serious about joining the team. Maybe even soccer-serious.

CindeeRae didn't say anything for a few seconds, and the crosswalk light went from red to white while we waited for her. "Oh, all right," she said, throwing her hands up. "But if you hurt anyone's feelings, or if you're pushy and rude, you're out!"

"Really?" Madeleine blinked, her cheeks flushing, like we had just offered to build her a fort of Oreos. She turned to CindeeRae and said, "I promise to be a good teammate."

March and I nodded. CindeeRae turned back to the road and yelled, "Walking man!"

The traffic signal blinked as the four of us crossed the intersection and continued on our way to Comic Warehouse.

CHAPTER FOUR

Comic Warehouse's entire storefront was covered by an illustration of a monstrous superhero. The muscles made the hero look bulky and awkward, with a tiny red cape barely covering his shoulders. His mouth was open, Cookie Monster–style, as he shoveled piles of comics down his gullet. Over the waiting stacks, *trash* was written in black spray paint.

The mural covered the old red brick of the warehouse, where buckets of paint now lined the wall. Miguel Martinez, owner of Comic Warehouse, assembled a paint roller, swearing under his breath about the vandal ruining the building's cool aesthetic. Now he'd have to paint over all the brick, and it would never look the same. Owen bent over the supplies, grabbing a paint tray for himself.

The thought of covering the comic-guzzling super-hero made the skin on my neck prickle. The painting was beautiful in a creepy, jagged way. The colors blended perfectly from red to purple with blue shading that reminded me of a real comic book. But I would never admit that to March. His face was flushed and his nostrils flared. Seeing the vandalization of a comic book store with his own eyeballs had turned him all ragey.

Madeleine stepped in front of Comic Warehouse, blocking everyone like she was warding off a mob, and said, "Can I take pictures before we start? You know, to document the damage?"

Miguel nodded, letting out a sigh that made him look smaller somehow. "I'm just thankful for your help." He shot Owen a crooked smile, which Owen didn't return. I looked at March to see if he felt the chilly energy pass between the two store owners, but March was gaping at the mural, each new detail seeming to make his wide eyes twitch.

I took a step toward Madeleine as she pulled her phone from her back pocket and roamed the length of the mural, snapping pictures from all angles. Every now and then she'd drop to her knee to get a better shot, and I watched her, nodding. She was a natural.

While we waited, I powered on my SleuthPad. A few months ago, I had spent all my paper route money on an iPad so I could digitize my detective files, which I had been keeping in a fancy notebook called the Sleuth Chronicle. Once we decided to work this case, I had saved the latest newspaper article about the vandal in a folder called Street Artist. Skimming the details from the story, I prepared to search the mural for evidence.

"There's got to be a clue here somewhere," I said to March and CindeeRae. "Pay attention to the details and look for anything out of place, especially a tag."

"A what?" CindeeRae asked.

"A tag," I said. "It's the way street artists sign their work."

"*Vandals*," March snapped. "It's the way *vandals* sign their work."

"Oh-kay." Madeleine had swung back to us and coughed into her fist: "Touchy."

CindeeRae narrowed her eyes at Madeleine. "Careful," she warned, looking ready to release some serious Shakespearean anger if our temporary teammate got even a little sassier.

"Okay, okay." Madeleine held her hands up in surrender.

"This is serious," March whispered, stepping between the two of them. "Owen's business is at stake, and maybe Miguel's, too. We need to be professional!"

Owen and Miguel had already started pouring white paint into the metal trays. "How's the Super Pickle these days?" Miguel asked as they began their work.

"It's never recovered since you opened *this* place, actually." Owen added an attachment to his paint roller and spun the fuzzy cover without looking at Miguel.

I cocked my head at March, murmuring, "You didn't tell us this happy reunion might end in a death match."

"They're fine," March said. "It's just friendly competition. But they put all bad feelings aside to fight the common enemy." It sounded like a comic book plot, and I imagined Owen and Miguel wearing capes as they battled the vandal with paint rollers.

The four of us split up to examine different parts of the mural, trying to find a clue in the details. I studied the superhero's upper body, looking for letters on his chest or initials hidden in his swirly blue-black hair. CindeeRae crouched below me, studying his knobby legs while Madeleine searched the yellow background. March squatted by the shaky tower of comic books, reading the thick spines with squinty eyes. Miguel and Owen were rolling their brushes over the far end of the mural, Miguel's speakers blaring songs from his own polka punk band.

"Are you guys going to help or what?" Owen asked, pausing to wipe his forehead with the back of his arm and leaving a long white streak along his hairline.

As if in response, March squealed, launching from his spot into a victory dance.

"What?" CindeeRae asked as he continued to spin in a lopsided circle, his elbows flapping up and down.

"I found a tag!" March stopped and puffed out his chest, arms outspread, as if he were waiting for someone to loop a medal around his neck. We all rushed to his side.

He pointed at the bottom of the stack, and everyone leaned in to try to unravel what looked like a doodle. After a couple seconds, the image snapped into focus, and I was able to recognize two letters in what looked like an ominous picture of a skull with pointy teeth: a capital *D* and *W*.

"Oh my gosh," Owen said, like we had just solved the case. Miguel looked equally stunned by March's discovery.

"What?" Madeleine asked. The four of us exchanged confused glances.

"Dark Writer," Owen said. "It's the symbol for Dark Writer."

"Who's Dark Writer?" March asked. This was starting to feel like a punch line to a joke the four of us couldn't possibly understand.

Miguel crossed his arms over his chest. "Dark Writer is a rare comic book series about a vigilante reporter, and that's his signature. I've never been able to get copies into Comic Warehouse, so that's all I know."

Owen nodded in agreement. "Me neither. It probably wasn't that popular in the first place, but every now and then I have someone request it."

"So Dark Writer is a comic book character?" Madeleine asked.

Miguel and Owen nodded.

"*And* the vandal targeting comic book stores?" she continued. "That doesn't make sense."

"Maybe it's just what he's calling himself," March said.

Miguel shook his head. "I have no idea what it means."

"Guess that's our first clue," Madeleine said as she took close-ups of the tag.

I followed the rest of the team to the paint supplies, grabbing a paint tray and roller of my own.

"It's not much of a clue." March shrugged.

"It will be once we figure out what it means," I said.

Miguel stood at the wall, holding the roller like he was afraid to take the first swipe at our clue. At last, he released a heaving sigh and rolled a narrow white swath over the stack of comic books.

CHAPTER FIVE

Madeleine sat with us at lunch on Monday, where the team talked about what to do with our one and only clue. Just a few seats down, our old lunch buddies, Jared Cramer and Pat Entler, talked about the new *Blood Eagle* opening at the theater that weekend.

March's eyes lit up when he heard them. "I can't wait!" he shouted. Then they all stretched over the long lunch table to exchange fist bumps. I only knew about Blood Eagle because it was a superhero series March was obsessed with; he had already sworn to drag me to the movie on Friday.

Cafeteria trays clanked as kids cleared their places, and the trade pile in the middle of our table dwindled. I had used sandwich crusts to re-create the vandal's Dark

Writer tag, and Madeleine snapped a picture of it with her phone, laughing.

"We should track down the Dark Writer comics, right?" Madeleine asked. CindeeRae rolled her eyes at the suggestion. I couldn't tell if it was because Madeleine's idea was obvious or because she thought Madeleine was being pushy.

"No fighting." March cleared his lunch garbage from the table, mumbling under his breath about how he had no time for amateurs. "If you want to solve the case, follow me. If you want to fight, take it behind the school." He pointed wildly in a direction that was not behind the school and then stomped out of the cafeteria holding folded newspapers under his arm like a businessman off to fire someone.

We shuffled to keep up as he ducked into the library and spread the newspapers onto a table against the back wall. Mrs. Davis, the school librarian, reshelved books while humming *The Price Is Right*'s theme song, which I only knew because Baa-chan's first weekend here, she had binged two weeks' worth of episodes in the basement. Madeleine, CindeeRae, and I sat in the small plastic chairs at the table, facing March like we were in a miniature board meeting.

"Kazu," March ordered. "Brief Madeleine on the case so we can get to work."

I thought about reminding him we were partners but

didn't feel like arguing with *this* March Winters. Besides, I had another case to manage; maybe it wasn't a bad idea if I let March think he was leading *this* investigation. He obviously had the passion for it.

I pulled the SleuthPad from under my arm and turned it on. Together Madeleine and I scrolled through the newspaper articles about the vandal hits: three in total, and all at Denver comic book stores. Aside from that and the Dark Writer tag at Comic Warehouse, we had no other clues.

"So, what do we know about Dark Writer?" CindeeRae asked.

In response, March held up a sheet of paper and read aloud: "'Dark Writer is a comic series about a reporter named Stan Wellerby who becomes the vigilante Dark Writer in order to uncover corruption among power-hungry superheroes.'" He looked up and shook his head. "That's all I could find."

"That doesn't give us much to go on," I said.

The library door clanged open, and Madeleine's best friend, Catelyn Monsen, stood in the entrance. She was with the new girl, Elesha Williams; the beads in Elesha's micro braids were still clicking.

We all twisted in our chairs to watch them, and I felt Madeleine stiffen at my side.

"Who hangs out in the library for lunch?" Catelyn asked Elesha, loud enough for everyone to hear.

Mrs. Davis shushed her. "The library is a wonderful place."

I studied Madeleine's expression, the corners of her mouth twitching. While no one knew why Madeleine had quit soccer, Catelyn Monsen was obviously mad about it. It didn't even look like they were best friends anymore.

CindeeRae turned back in her seat and flipped her long red hair over her shoulder. "Mean people suck," she muttered under her breath. I couldn't tell if she was commiserating with Madeleine or condemning her.

Catelyn and Elesha left as suddenly as they'd come with another clang of the library door, and March snapped his fingers to get our attention. Sheesh! Acting Lead Investigator Winters was pushy and impatient. Madeleine shifted in her seat, and CindeeRae gave her a side glance before squaring her shoulders, her back straight.

But before March could continue, Mrs. Davis stepped up to our table hugging a small stack of books to her chest. Her golden-brown skin glowed against her coral dress. "I couldn't help but overhear that you're looking for information."

March's nose bunched up. "We don't need book information, exactly."

I jumped in. "We need comic book information, specifically."

"What I meant *was*," March said, wresting the

conversation back from me, "is the information we need won't be found in a book. It'll probably be in some obscure archive online."

Mrs. Davis leaned over and lowered her voice like she was sharing a secret. "You may be surprised to learn that I actually know a thing or two about obscure archives. Online *and* in books."

March drew his eyebrows together. Then he said, "I think we're okay."

"Not so fast," I interrupted again, feeling like March was letting this lead investigator thing go to his head. "We might need your help. It's just that, right now, we're not even sure what we're looking for."

"Okay." Mrs. Davis cradled the books with one hand while grabbing her glasses from where they rested on a chain around her neck. She slid them back on. "You know where to find me if you think I can help."

CindeeRae waited until Mrs. Davis had moved far enough away, then whispered, "That was *rude,* March."

"We just don't need her help," March said, looking at me to back him up. I raised my eyebrows and shook my head.

"Whatever," he huffed, rolling his newspapers and fixing them under his arm. "Meet at my house after school tomorrow. I have an idea for tracking down Dark Writer comics."

"Why not today?" Madeleine asked.

Dropping his stern, lead-detective face, March said, "It's Sorcery Night at the Super Pickle."

We all nodded, and March's expression hardened again. "Tomorrow. After school."

"Yes, sir!" I saluted, hoping to break the tension. No one even smiled.

• • •

A big mystery package arrived from Japan that afternoon, but Baa-chan didn't open it until that night. "Can I help you open it, Okaa-san?" Dad asked when she went into the living room with a box cutter.

We had just finished loading the dishwasher, and Dad stood in the kitchen doorway drying his hands on a towel. I padded toward the stairs, ready to search for more information on Dark Writer in my room. Genki followed me, his nails clicking on the tile floor.

"Kazuko-chan will help," Baa-chan said.

I stopped and slowly turned around. Dad shrugged. A hard stone formed in my throat as I walked over to Baa-chan. Why did she need *me* to help her? I had already finished a long list of chores she had given me after school, including digging all the dead leaves and grass from the flower bed we never use in the backyard.

I stood in front of her, my arms folded tightly across my chest. Genki looked between the two of us like we were planning him a party, his tail swishing expectantly.

"Please move that table." She motioned at the side table by the couch and then waved her hand at the fireplace.

I moved the table to the fireplace and then turned back to Baa-chan, who was pulling a smaller box from inside the first. The silence in the room throbbed in my ears, and I wondered how long this would take. Genki finally decided to get comfortable, turning a few circles before dropping onto the small shag rug in front of the fireplace.

Using the box cutter again, Baa-chan slit open the second box and tried hefting something from inside, but it wouldn't budge. She set it back on the floor and pointed at the bottom of the box. "Hold on," she said, tipping it back and wrestling with the contents. I sat with my legs straddling the bottom as she pulled.

Slowly, a Styrofoam rectangle slid out. When it sprang from the cardboard, Baa-chan staggered back, and the box almost hit my face. I hooted with laughter. She cut me a look before breaking into a smile and then releasing a quick chortle that sounded like a burp.

Baa-chan opened the two halves of Styrofoam to

reveal a stone statue the size of a garden gnome. She set it onto the table and stood back to admire it. "We'll move it to the patch you cleared today after we plant a few flowers. It'll look perfect out there."

I cocked my head to the side, studying what looked like a monk standing with his hands pressed together. He was bald, his eyes closed and his lips turned up in a small smile.

"What is it?" I asked.

"O-jizō-sama," she said, like I knew what that meant. Then she looked at me and explained, "He's the Buddhist protector of children and babies."

I wanted to ask why she brought him here, but I knew that no matter how I phrased the question, it would sound rude. Instead, I decided to study the statue for exactly thirty seconds before heading to my room so I didn't seem disrespectful.

Baa-chan interrupted my countdown. "I got this for your mother," she said. "I thought it might help her feel better."

My face twisted in confusion, and I was torn between fleeing the conversation and finding out exactly how a Japanese lawn ornament would help Mom feel better.

"Why?" The word tumbled from my mouth, jagged at the edges.

Baa-chan sighed as if she were ready to flee this

conversation, too. "We'll talk about it more when your mother's ready." She gathered the boxes and added, "You should go up and finish your homework."

Now that she was giving me permission to leave, I wanted to stay and learn more. But the moment for asking questions had already passed. Instead, I left the room without saying anything, Genki's footfalls light behind me.

CHAPTER SIX

My alarm went off at five forty-five the next morning, fifteen minutes before I was supposed to do the paper route. It was time for Operation Identify Mom's Physician. I planned to search her phone to find out more about her doctor. If I knew why she had been seeing one in the first place, I might better understand what was wrong with her now. Then maybe I could fix it so she could be my mom again.

Even though it was early spring, my bedroom windows were still black with night. I held my arms out as I made my way to the doorway, and leaving the lights off, peeked into the hallway to see if my parents' door was still open. I dropped to my knees and Genki leaned against me. He yawned loudly into my ear, and I shushed him.

Dad's snoring echoed from their bedroom. The bathroom light poured into the hallway and through their open door, lighting a patch of carpet in their room. I crawled toward it, cutting Genki a warning look as we padded along. When I paused at the foot of their bed, Genki pushed his snout into my ribs, like he had been briefed on this particular operation and knew it was his job to hurry me along. I glared at him and dropped flat on the floor, commando-crawling to Mom's nightstand.

The phone rested facedown next to her alarm clock, and as I snatched it from the tabletop the screen lit up and seemed to set the room aglow. I dropped the phone to my chest and smothered the light while Mom released a long sigh and rolled over. I lay there for a few seconds, waiting for my heart to stop racing. Genki dipped his head toward me and blew air through his floppy jowls; in the quiet room, the sound seemed louder than a fire alarm.

I rose to my knees just as I heard Mom mumble, "Genki, what are you doing in here?"

I froze, my heart pounding in my chest. Genki's head rested on Mom's side of the bed, his tail beating the nightstand as it wagged happily.

I inched backward and watched Mom lazily scratch at Genki's ear with closed eyes. "Wake up Kazu, boy," she muttered. "She's going to be late for the paper route. Go!"

Instead of leaving like a good dog, Genki barked. *Traitor.*

She lifted her head to peer through the dark room and saw me squatting on the floor.

"Kazu?" she asked sleepily. "What are you doing in here?"

I slipped Mom's phone into my pj's pocket before she could notice it. "Genki snuck into your room on our way to do the route." I yawned like I hadn't been in the middle of a sneaky operation. "Come on, you big doofus." I yanked on Genki's collar and pulled him from the room, wondering how I could return the phone before Mom realized it was missing.

• • •

After the paper route, I sat cross-legged in the middle of my room and searched Mom's calendar. Genki had dropped to the floor in front of me dramatically, as if getting up fifteen minutes early had been too much for him. The sound of his panting filled the room as I studied Mom's phone.

Her calendar had been crowded with monthly doctor appointments since the beginning of the year. An icy chill flooded my body. Healthy people didn't see the doctor this much, I thought. Maybe she had been sick long before Baa-chan had come.

The appointments were generic, without a doctor's name or address, so I opened her contacts and did a search for "Dr." Mom's phone displayed three listings: Dr. Slade, Dr. Phillips, and Dr. Bassi. I took a picture of the contact information for each with my SleuthPad and dropped the phone into my back pocket just as Baa-chan's voice sounded up the stairs.

"Kazuko-chan! You're late already. Hurry!"

I scrambled up and grabbed my backpack.

"Coming," I called back as I tiptoed to Mom's now-closed bedroom door. It creaked as I opened it, and Mom smiled at me weakly when I peeked inside. She was sitting up in bed, pillows propped behind her, with a TV tray on her lap.

"Kazu." She waved me over, and when I reached her bedside, she pulled me into a half hug. "Baa-chan has a routine she likes me to follow, and it begins with a breakfast I mostly don't eat. Help me out?"

The phone sat heavy in my back pocket. I tried to ignore the constriction around my heart as I popped a melon ball into my mouth.

"You should eat the toast, too." She pushed the plate toward me. Even though I'd probably get in trouble with Baa-chan for not eating my own breakfast, I scarfed down the honeyed toast and brushed the crumbs from my mouth.

"Love you, Mom," I said, bending over to kiss her cheek. I slipped the phone from my pocket and back onto her nightstand.

"Love you, too, sweetie," she said. "And could you take the tray down with you?" She was already sinking back under the covers.

I nodded and carried the tray down the stairs.

But when I came into the kitchen, Baa-chan seemed distracted by something; I looked closer and saw a framed picture nearly hidden between the cabinets and the back door. "What's this?" She walked to the picture and touched the frame gently. It was a watercolor I had painted of a beach, the salt sprinkled along the sandy shore making the sand look like tiny crystals glistening in the sun.

"Just something I made in art class."

As if my words had cast a spell, Baa-chan's expression softened from disapproval to delight. "Art was my favorite subject in school."

"Really?"

"I loved making paper collages." She held out her hand as if wielding an imaginary paintbrush. "I'd mix Japanese calligraphy with washi, stamps, and original artwork." Who was this lady? Her expression was dreamy and made her practically unrecognizable.

"Watercolor is *my* favorite," I said. "We did a series of nature paintings, and this is Seaside Beach, from a trip we took to Oregon last summer."

"Watercolor is beautiful, too," she said, but as she turned to look at me again, her eyes snagged on the clock and her brows drew together. "You will miss the bus!"

I put the TV tray next to the sink and ran to the door to find my shoes and backpack. Baa-chan handed me two lunch sacks.

When I looked at her, puzzled, she said, "One is lunch, the other breakfast, since we were running late."

I nodded, smiling, and shot out the door as Genki sat obediently next to Baa-chan, watching me go. "Good-bye," I called as I ran through our yard, and then my brain scrambled to think of something she might like even more. Almost too late for Baa-chan to hear, I called out some Japanese Mom had taught me when I was younger. "Ittekimasu." "I will go and come back."

"Itterasshai." The word echoed behind me: "Go and return."

I looked back and waved so she would know I had heard.

CHAPTER SEVEN

March sat at his desk while CindeeRae, Madeleine, and I lay on the floor of his bedroom, hovering over my SleuthPad. CindeeRae was showing us different interpretations of the Ladybug character in her play while March read another Blood Eagle comic. We had come to his house to track down a lead but had quickly been distracted by CindeeRae's obsession with her role as the motherly beetle.

Madeleine rolled over and stared at the ceiling. "Can we get started already? I mean, dramatic ladybugs are great and all, but . . ."

"Just this last one," CindeeRae said, flashing us an image of a girl in a puffy red dress with black polka dots. Her black hat had pipe-cleaner antennae springing from the top. I rolled onto my back, too, and together Madeleine and I studied the constellation painted on March's ceiling.

"Okay, I'm done," CindeeRae said, closing the browser window and reopening my Street Artist folder.

"Earth to March," I said. He held up a finger. I let out a huff and snapped, "If CindeeRae searches 'ladybug' again, we'll never get any work done."

CindeeRae cut her eyes at me, but just as quickly shrugged it off. "Are you still reading that?" she asked March. He had been carrying a small stack of Blood Eagle comics with him all day, even to lunch.

"I just want to read the series again before the movie premiere."

Madeleine stood up and peered over his shoulder at the comic. "So you're reading the most recent version and not Phoenix Rising's first edition?"

Because this was one of March's favorite comics, I knew that Blood Eagle had two versions. The first edition was dark and gritty. But then they redesigned the series for a bigger audience. That's when Blood Eagle exploded and became so popular they decided to make a movie, which was opening this weekend.

"The first edition is expensive." March looked up and blinked at Madeleine. "I don't know *anyone* who has the first edition, including Owen. And how do you even know about that?"

Madeleine dropped into the kiddie-size beanbag chair that was covered in rocketships and next to March's desk. She grinned. "I told you I'm a comic book geek. But I've only read the one the movie is based on." She shook her head. "It would be *so* cool to read the first edition, though."

"Right?" March rested his head against the chairback, having forgotten the comic splayed on his lap. "I would love to get my hands on those."

I looked from Madeleine to March blankly, feeling comic-overload. "So, what exactly is our mission today?"

March sighed, looking lost in his vision of first edition comics, and then said, "There's a discussion board called GeekReader, where you post questions, and super geeks around the world answer them. I thought we could see if anyone there knows where to find Dark Writer comics."

CindeeRae sat up and crossed her legs. "You think if we read the comics, we'll figure out who the vandal is?"

"In the three hits so far, it's the only solid clue we have," I said. "There's got to be some connection—a reason our vandal would sign the name of a comic book character to his graffiti."

"Cool plan." Madeleine shifted deeper into the beanbag and added, "Maybe someone on GeekReader could sell us a first edition Blood Eagle, too."

March turned to face his computer and began typing something into the search bar. He clicked madly at the keypad as he logged onto the discussion board.

"Does anyone know," he read aloud as he typed his post for GeekReader, "where we could find issues of the Dark Writer comics?" He spun back in the chair to look at us. "How does that sound?"

"I bet Dark Writer is a street artist, and that's why the vandal's using his tag," CindeeRae said. "Maybe we could ask?"

March steepled his hands, poised to lecture her. "We're dealing with geeks skimming a discussion board. We cram too much in there, and they won't even read the post. Short and simple is the best approach." He nodded his head slowly. "Trust me."

"Whoever it is hates comics," Madeleine said.

I nodded. Targeting three comic book stores had definitely made that clear.

While March launched into a discussion on the criminal profiles of serial street artists, I snuck into another folder on my SleuthPad to view the picture I had taken earlier for my second, secret case—Mission: Mom Recovery. I needed to do some research on the list of doctors I had gotten from her phone: Dr. Slade, Dr. Bassi, and Dr. Phillips. I already knew that Dr. Phillips was my pediatrician, so Mom couldn't have been seeing her. Just as I ran a search on Dr. Slade, I heard March clear his throat.

I snapped my head up to find him, Madeleine, and CindeeRae staring at me. "Sorry," I said. "Just thinking about the case." And it wasn't even a lie.

March's exasperation leaked out in a sigh. He turned back to his computer and waved at the screen. "I was hoping someone would answer right away. But it looks like we might have to wait a few days until we hear back."

"What do we do until then?" Madeleine asked.

"At some point," March said, "we may want to search for our vandal's practice site."

"Practice what?" CindeeRae asked.

"That mural on Comic Warehouse was huge," March explained. "To make something that big without getting caught means the vandal probably practices somewhere, over and over again, before the actual hit. The better they get, the less time it takes. They do that at a practice site."

"Professor Winters." I rolled my eyes. "Could we please be excused?"

"Sorry." He shrugged. "I've done a lot of research on graffiti lately because I thought it would help. Besides, who said searching for clues takes a lot of time, and if you don't have the patience, you should leave?"

It was like March and I had switched roles, and it was making me snappish. "I don't know, Sherlock. Who?"

"You!" he scoffed. "To Madeleine when she first joined our team."

"He's right," Madeleine said, standing. "You did say that."

"All right, all right." I stood, too, ready to end this team meeting. "We wait until we have more clues."

Already my mind was flitting back to my other case.

CHAPTER EIGHT

The next day after school, Madeleine stood at my front door, her bike on the ground in my drive-way like she was in a hurry. "I know what March said about being patient," she said. Genki stuck his head from behind me, and Madeleine scratched it while she talked. "But this is a mini emergency. Comic Relief looks like they're about ready to paint over their graffiti, and I thought we could hurry over and get pictures before they cover it up. You know, close-ups."

Apparently, on their way home from running errands, Madeleine and her mom had just passed one of the other two comic book stores struck by the vandal, and the mural was still a glaring addition to the storefront. But it didn't look like it would last much longer.

"Someone had just put down a tarp and brought out paint cans. So, if we wait too long, it'll be gone by the time we get there."

"Should I call March and CindeeRae?" I asked.

"I don't think we have time," she said, her hands twisting together. "Plus, it'd probably take a while to convince March why we should go in the first place."

She was right. March Winters, acting lead investigator, was all about thinking long and hard before following leads. After our last meeting, he definitely seemed more interested in waiting for clues to turn up instead of tracking them down ourselves. And if Comic Relief had just put down a tarp, they were probably already painting. That mural could be gone in a matter of minutes.

"Let me grab my SleuthPad and Genki's harness."

Madeleine followed me into the house, and I introduced her to Baa-chan in the kitchen while I grabbed the leash from the broom closet.

"Is it okay if we go on a quick bike ride?" I asked.

"Take the nine-one-one phone and be home by dinner." Baa-chan called the emergency flip phone my parents had gotten me the 9-1-1 phone, which seemed appropriate.

Madeleine and I rushed out to the garage with Genki, where I grabbed my bike and followed her through the neighborhood toward West Highland. Comic Relief was just down the street from Magic Planet, the abandoned amusement park that was being renovated into a botanical garden and outdoor shopping mall.

The afternoon was warm enough to heat my cheeks, but the cool air of spring still bit at my fingers. Genki pounded the pavement next to me, and after about ten minutes we pulled into the parking lot of Comic Relief.

"Wait!" Madeleine yelled, stopping a teenage boy from rolling white paint over the bottom corner of the mural. The kid pushed his glasses up the bridge of his nose with the back of his hand and watched us while we parked our bikes and walked to where he stood on the tarp.

"Can we take pictures?" Madeleine asked. "We're investigating the vandal's activities and were hoping to secure some evidence." She talked like a detective sent by the police department. I side-eyed her, feeling like she was a little too comfortable playing lead investigator herself.

"Oh, sure," he said, stepping back and putting his roller in the paint tray. "I was going to grab a soda anyway."

The kid went inside Comic Relief and left Madeleine and me on the tarp in front of the mural. It was a ginormous garbage dump filled with stacks and stacks of comic books. The piles in front were taller than Madeleine and me, towering nearly to the top of the store, while the ones in back were tiny and narrow. The image was imposing, filled with as much anger as comics. Our vandal wasn't doing this for fun; he was enraged. If only we could figure out why.

Genki began to paw at the blue plastic, looking to make himself comfortable with a tarp nest, but I stopped him before he reached the paint tray. I stood back to take a picture with my SleuthPad, pulling Genki with me, while Madeleine got to work capturing the mural from all sides, dropping to her knees to get close-ups of the comic stacks, where you could even read names and publishers on the spines.

"Where did you learn to take pictures?" I watched images freeze on her screen as she moved down the wall to catch sections of the painting.

"My grandpa taught me a little," she said. "He's a photographer, and I've always liked watching him work."

I studied the graffiti as Madeleine worked quietly, Genki pulling his leash as he tried to follow her down the wall. After she passed in front of me, I stepped up to the mural and used my hands to walk through each section, like it was a ginormous hidden-object puzzle. I ignored the comic books and instead searched the land-fill trash for another tag, which was mostly a bunch of squiggly lines. But when I reached the center of the picture, I found a soda can with an image on it.

"Madeleine." My voice squeaked.

She turned, her eyebrows raised.

"Another Dark Writer tag," I said, my voice a low murmur.

She rushed to where I stood, and her mouth dropped open. There it was, the *DW* on the soda can, looking like the sign for poison.

"They're definitely connected," Madeleine finally said. "Like, we know the same person did the two murals, and this second tag proves there's a connection to the Dark Writer comic. I bet there was a Dark Writer tag on Mile High Comics, too."

I nodded, feeling both thrilled and guilty at the discovery. We'd have to share it with March and CindeeRae, who wouldn't be happy that we'd found it on our own.

Madeleine took a close-up of the tag, then stood back a few feet and snapped another picture. "This is huge." She slipped her phone into her back pocket and walked to our bikes. "I'll have my dad print the pictures tonight, and we can talk about them tomorrow."

"March isn't going to be happy about it," I said. I imagined the twisty look of his face when he felt hurt or betrayed.

"We wouldn't have found it if we hadn't come right away," she said, pushing up the kickstand and swinging a leg over her ten-speed. "He can't be mad at us for finding an important clue."

Still, the pinch of guilt spread through my stomach and swelled in my throat as we pedaled home. Madeleine was right. We wouldn't have found this clue if we had waited to include March and CindeeRae. But it wasn't just about finding clues. It was about feeling like a team, and I knew that March would be more upset that we hadn't included him than he would about not okaying this mission as lead investigator.

I suddenly realized that having a four-person detective team was going to be harder than I ever imagined.

CHAPTER NINE

Mom was eating dinner with us for the first time in a couple of weeks. While we waited for the food to be ready, Genki and I sprawled on the living room rug, resting from our late afternoon trip to Comic Relief. Our stomachs growled as we listened to the chicken pop in the boiling oil. Baa-chan was cooking Mom's favorite childhood dish—chicken karaage, which is basically Japanese fried chicken, only much better than any American version I'd ever tried.

Smoke from the incense Baa-chan had lit next to O-jizō-sama swirled over us, and the musky scent made me sleepy. I turned to my side, resting my head on my arm, and studied the friendly monk statue. His smile was comforting; he looked like he had everything figured out, or was okay with things as they were. I wasn't sure if I could ever be that calm, at least not with unsolved mysteries in my life. With that thought, the anxious knot about Mom's mystery sickness tightened in my chest, and I curled around Genki, hoping to snuggle it away.

At last, Baa-chan called everyone to dinner. When Genki followed me to the table, she shooed him into the garage to eat his dry, pebbly meal.

I could hear Mom trudging down the stairs. When she came through the living room, she stopped for a second and stared at the O-jizō-sama. She walked to the table he rested on and brushed her fingers over his bald head. I heard her release a jagged sigh before continuing to the table, where all the adults sat like they were holding their breath.

I looked from Dad to Mom to Baa-chan, waiting for someone to spill the bad news.

"What's wrong?" I asked. We should all be smiling and chatting happily to celebrate Mom coming downstairs. Plus, karaage!

"Nothing," Dad said a little too quickly. "We're just eating dinner together as a family." He sounded like a guy selling family dinners.

Mom nodded, her face a little pale and her hair still bed-rumpled. Baa-chan smiled nervously. The silence became so heavy it hummed, until we heard Genki scratching at the garage door, asking to be let back in.

Baa-chan bellowed, "Stop, Genki," and even Mom jumped a little bit.

I picked up my chopsticks, clicking them together in one hand as I waited for the go-ahead to dig into the plate piled high with fried chicken pieces.

Baa-chan frowned at me and then raised her eyebrows.

"What?" I looked from Baa-chan to Mom, wishing grown-ups would just say what they meant.

"Manners," Baa-chan said. I stopped clicking my chopsticks and waited until she finally said, "Please eat."

I pushed my dish next to the karaage and shoveled chicken pieces onto my plate with my chopsticks. The quiet made me nervous, so I filled the silence with chatter. "I'm so glad you've finally come down from your room, Mom. Things just haven't been the same, and it looks like you're feeling so much better—"

A hand slammed onto the table between my plate and the serving dish, hitting the tips of my chopsticks and flinging them onto the floor. "Don't be rude, Kazuko!" Mom's voice was deep and low, which some-how made it more terrifying. "You don't heap food onto your plate like that."

I leaned back in my seat, as far from her as I could get. Dad looked at me, his expression soft and sad. He got up, grabbed my chopsticks from the floor, and walked into the kitchen.

Mom rarely yelled at me like that. She would get frustrated and upset by some of the things I did, but this response was different. It was scary. As if she could read my mind, Mom's face fell, her eyes filling with tears. She reached out and covered my hand with hers, and I could feel the pulse in her palm. "I'm so sorry, Kazu."

I wrenched my fingers free and folded my hands in my lap. "I didn't mean to be rude," I said.

Baa-chan nodded and leaned forward to dish broccoli onto my plate. Then she scooped a serving of sticky rice from the rice cooker and plopped it next to my pile of karaage. "Dōzo," she said, telling me to go ahead and eat. Even though it was one simple Japanese word, she said it so tenderly that my eyes stung.

Dad returned to the dining room, Genki at his heels, and handed me a clean pair of chopsticks. He winked and said, "Eat up, Bug."

My appetite was gone, even though Genki licked at my toes under the table, reminding me that our mouths had been watering over the karaage just an hour ago.

Mom seemed to be taking deep, soothing breaths, as if the whole episode had triggered a panic attack. Baa-chan placed her hand over Mom's on the table. It was like watching two people share a secret handshake.

Finally, Mom seemed to compose herself, and she asked, "So how was your day, Kazu?" She crumpled the napkin she had used to dab at her eyes in a tight fist.

I shrugged. "Good, I guess." Silence filled the room again. It felt like our family dinner was actually an audition for more family dinners. So I started talking. "We had a team meeting at March's house about the vandal case, and we're looking for these really rare comics that are currently our only clue, but we have no idea whether they'll help us at all once we find them. And March thinks we need to be patient and wait for some answers instead of trying to figure out a different plan, and since I've let him be in charge for the first time ever, I need to give him his bossy space. . . ."

"Kazu-chan, slow down," Baa-chan said. I looked up, and Baa-chan and Dad were staring at me. "You can tell us about your case, but eat a little, talk a little."

I sighed and steadied my chopsticks with shaky fingers, suddenly regretting all the chicken I had piled onto my plate. I took a bite and chewed, and the sound seemed to roar in the silent dining room. After I swallowed, I began telling Baa-chan all about our case while she nodded her understanding, a small smile on her lips reminding me of O-jizō-sama. Even still, I was pretty sure I had failed the audition.

CHAPTER TEN

The next morning, everything went wrong. I woke up late and had to finish the paper route in thirty minutes. Genki, who's usually my focused guardian, saw a squirrel in Mrs. Fitzman's ficus and chased it through all the backyards on the south side of Colonial until he got stuck in Mr. McMurry's yard with the high corner fence. By the time we got home, breakfast was cold and Baa-chan had to call Dad back from his work commute to drive me to school because I had already missed the bus.

And it was only when Dad stopped to let me out in front of the school that I realized I was still wearing my pajama top, which featured a ginormous picture of Scooby-Doo gobbling up pizza slices, and the words

Sweet dreams are made of cheese. Which may not have been *that* bad except it was probably three sizes too small, the cuffs cutting off at my elbows and the hem barely touching the waistband of my pants.

"Can't you take me home to change?" I asked Dad, ducking back into the car.

"Bug, I'm already *very* late to work."

"But I didn't even bring a jacket," I whined. I wasn't much of a fashionista, but even *I* knew fifth grade was *way* too old to be wearing toddler-size pajamas with cartoons on them.

"Sorry, Kazu." He looked at his watch for emphasis. "I've got to run."

I shut the car door and slogged to the front of the school, my backpack feeling like it was loaded with rocks. Even so, if I carried it around all day, maybe no one would notice my Scooby pajamas. Just as I was wondering whether or not Mrs. Thomas would let me wear my backpack in class, Madeleine spooked me at the top of the stairs, waving a stack of papers.

"I got the printouts," Madeleine said. When I didn't answer, she rushed to say, "I thought we could study them with the team at lunch. They'll be happy as soon as they realize we can prove the two murals are connected to each other *and* Dark Writer."

I took the papers from her and held them over the front of my shirt. "Can I borrow them?" I asked, not sure if I wanted to study the pictures for clues or use them as a shield.

"Of course!" Madeleine said as she walked toward Mr. Carter's class. "Just bring them with you to the cafeteria."

I stepped into Mrs. Thomas's class right before the tardy bell rang.

"What took you so long?" CindeeRae hollered at me from her seat. She squinted when I went straight to our desks. "Aren't you going to put your backpack on the hook?"

"Nope." I settled into my seat and was suddenly very squished, the backpack pushing my stomach into the desk.

"Oh-kay," CindeeRae mumbled from her spot behind me.

Mrs. Thomas called the class to attention. As she marked the roll, her eyes caught on me. "Kazu, could you please hang your backpack on the hook?"

I groaned. "No, thank you?"

Mrs. Thomas liked me, and for the first year in my entire academic career I had been in hardly any trouble at school. So her look of surprise when I didn't obey her was almost a compliment. "Backpacks go on hooks," she said sternly, nodding at the list of Classroom Courtesies that had been hanging on the wall all year.

I didn't want to be caught wearing my baby pj's at

school, but I didn't want Mrs. Thomas to be mad at me even more. So I stood and walked to the hook as everyone watched. I set the papers on the craft table so I could hang my backpack on the wall. As I did, giggles erupted from the back corner of the class, Catelyn Monsen cackling the loudest before saying, "Kazu wants some Scooby Snacks." Then the whole class was laughing. I snatched the papers back to my chest and returned to my desk. Mrs. Thomas looked at me apologetically, and that almost made it worse.

None of this would have happened if Mom wasn't sick, I thought angrily. If she hadn't been locked in her bedroom this morning, she would have noticed I wasn't up for my route on time and would have woken me. I would have come home to eat a warm breakfast and make the bus. And before I headed out the door, she would have laughed at my Scooby pj's and shooed me back to change.

And just as quickly, I felt guilty. Mom was only acting different because she was sick. Solving my second case suddenly became much more important. It was time to discover which of the doctors she had been seeing before catching the bedroom sickness. If I could figure out why she was going to the doctor every month before Baa-chan had come, maybe it would help me discover what was wrong with her now.

Time to complete Operation Identify Mom's Physician.

• • •

On my way out of the bathroom after lunch, I caught Madeleine slipping from the library and followed her to the empty four-square court behind the school, where we were holding a team meeting during recess. March and CindeeRae each sat in their own square. I surrendered the printouts I had been carrying all morning and spread them on the concrete, eyeing Madeleine as I did. What had she been doing in the library alone?

"Where were you?" March asked.

I smoothed my shirt over my belly after I sat on the ground. "I was in the bathroom," I said.

"I just had to grab something from the library," Madeleine said, and then cocked her head to study my pj top. I crossed my arms over my chest.

March leaned toward the pictures and asked, "What is all this?"

"I printed off pictures from all the hits," Madeleine said. "We only have the newspaper's close-up of the toilet from Mile High Comics, since they already covered it. But Kazu and I were able to take close-ups of the landfill mural at Comic Relief yesterday, right before they started painting."

A quick look passed between March and CindeeRae. March's mouth straightened into a tight line. "You went to Comic Relief without us?"

"They were literally getting ready to paint over it when my mom and I drove by. So I rushed over to tell Kazu," Madeleine said, but I could tell from her tone that she didn't realize how serious this was to March. "We would have missed it if we had waited for everyone."

CindeeRae looked at March and then squared her shoulders at us. "We're a team," she said. "You should have at least let us know what you were doing."

"But we're telling you now," Madeleine said. She looked at them, her face set in an expression that reminded me of Madeleine Brown the bully. I touched her arm hoping she'd back down.

March scoffed and looked away, while CindeeRae leaned back on her arms.

I pulled the most important picture from the stack and set it in front of them, hoping we could forget about this disagreement and be a team again.

"You found another Dark Writer tag?" March asked. He snatched the picture from the ground and held it to his nose.

"Yep," Madeleine said. "I just don't get it. Who hates comics this much, but then names themselves after a comic book character?"

CindeeRae nodded, adding, "And what would make them mad enough to lash out at comic book stores?"

"That's interesting and everything." March waved

away the picture like he was waving away their questions. "But we shouldn't get distracted by *why* the vandal's mad. Instead we need to focus on *who* he is. That's like Batman getting distracted by the wrong thing in the Riddler's riddles."

Madeleine gave March a pointed look. "Well, that's stupid," she said. "Finding out *why* he's mad might tell us *who* he is."

"Hey, be nice." CindeeRae's eyebrows shot up at Madeleine's critical tone. "We'll keep the vandal's motive in mind as we move forward, okay? Since we don't have much to go on right now, *any* clues will help."

"We just need to see what's in the Dark Writer comics," March said. "There's got to be a clue on what he's planning to do next."

"And our next agenda item," Madeleine said as March lifted himself from the pavement, ready to leave. "The *Blood Eagle* movie. We should all go watch it together."

CindeeRae beamed. "I don't have rehearsal on Friday, so I'm free."

"I just got a new BE shirt to wear," March said, his irritation over our rogue mission temporarily forgotten.

I breathed a sigh of relief.

"BE shirt?" CindeeRae asked.

"Blood Eagle," Madeleine and March sang out in unison. Madeleine laughed and then held out her hands for high fives.

"Or," March said, already too distracted to high-five her back, "I could wear the wings!"

"I'm in!" I halfheartedly met Madeleine's hand with my own.

The bell rang. CindeeRae folded up the papers and held them toward me.

"Thanks, but they're Madeleine's." I had been using them as a shield all day but had become almost more self-conscious of holding the pictures over my shirt than I was of the actual pajama top.

As we walked toward the fifth-grade line for the side door, Madeleine leaned toward me and whispered, "Do you want to borrow my jacket?" She wore a gray wind-breaker with red piping. "It's warm today, and I don't need it."

"Are you sure?" I whispered back.

"Yep." She shrugged off the jacket and handed it to me. "And you don't have to bring it back until tomorrow."

I mumbled thanks and slipped the jacket on, zipping it up halfway. She smiled back, and I ducked my head, not sure why such a nice gesture made me want to cry.

CHAPTER ELEVEN

I lay on my bedroom floor next to Genki, dirty clothes strewn about the room, and began searching the doctors listed in Mom's phone. I had already ruled out Dr. Phillips, my pediatrician, so I focused on the two remaining doctors: Dr. Slade and Dr. Bassi.

Using my SleuthPad, I looked up Dr. Slade in the Denver area and found two listings. One was an acupuncturist and the other an ob-gyn. I checked them against the phone number from the picture, and Dr. William Slade was a match.

What was an ob-gyn anyway?

Genki stood and reassessed his spot before circling a couple of times farther down and dropping to the floor again, the bulk of his weight on my legs.

"Hey!" I said, scissoring them until he shifted mostly off my body, resting his head on my thigh instead.

I continued my research and found out that ob-gyn was the abbreviation for *obstetrics and gynecology*, which didn't help me at all. After clicking a few more links I realized that an ob-gyn was the doctor who helped women have babies.

A baby doctor? Mom hadn't needed one of those since I was born. I sighed at this second dead end and turned my attention to Dr. Bassi.

My bedroom door opened, and I startled at the sound, scaring Genki from his spot. He stood facing Baa-chan with a growl rumbling in his throat.

"What are you doing up here all alone?" She still wore her apron from dinner and her short, dark hair was tousled, like she had just run around the block.

"Working on homework." I tilted my SleuthPad so she couldn't see the screen.

"Are you supposed to be on that all night?" she asked, nodding at the device.

I understood that Baa-chan was my substitute mom right now, but the question annoyed me. "I have parental controls." My voice was sharper than I'd intended. "They filter out bad stuff and set limits on my internet activity."

Baa-chan nodded slowly. "I think you should probably work at the table," she said. "I'll keep you company."

"Can't I just finish what I'm doing right now?"

"I'll see you in ten minutes." She spun around without waiting for me to respond, leaving the door gaping behind her.

I grumbled to myself as I turned back to my SleuthPad, which had gone to sleep since Baa-chan had barged in. Genki watched me for a few seconds as I woke it back up, and then he spun a circle before dropping back onto my legs. Even my nosy mother let me study alone in my room, I thought as I typed *Doctor Bassi* into the search bar with a stabby finger.

There was only one result: Dr. Amoli Bassi, a neurologist downtown. Seeing that I only had eight minutes to get downstairs, I ran another quick search on *neurologist* and discovered that it was a doctor specializing in disorders and diseases of the nervous system. In science this year, Mrs. Thomas had spent one day covering the nervous system, which I just remember being a tangle of tiny channels that carried physical sensations throughout the body. We had talked for a while about a kid she had known who didn't feel any pain. His parents hardly allowed him to do anything, because he could break an arm and not even know it. Mrs. Thomas explained that he had a nerve disease. Was Mom suffering from something like that?

"Kazu-chan!" Baa-chan yelled from the bottom of the stairs, and I shook Genki off my legs to stand, clutching my SleuthPad, and this new information, to my chest.

● ● ●

Mrs. Davis waved us over to the library as we spilled from the cafeteria that Friday. We followed her to the back table, where she had set up a school iPad and an open magazine.

"Madeleine asked me to do a little research on a comic book you're investigating." She pushed her glasses down on her nose so she could look at us over the rims. "Dark Writer?"

March shot Madeleine a glare and then folded his arms across his chest, covering the new Blood Eagle shirt he had worn for the movie premiere that night. Madeleine wore one, too, although hers was a vintage style. Both had a sprawling picture of Blood Eagle on the front with his majestic, arching wings, only they looked more skeletal on Madeleine's shirt—sharp and ominous.

Madeleine ignored March and turned all her attention to the librarian. "I just thought that Mrs. Davis might be able to find something about Dark Writer."

While I didn't agree with Madeleine going to Mrs. Davis on her own, I did think it was okay to ask for help when you got stuck. In fact, it wasn't just okay, it was good detecting. "It can't hurt to gather more information until we hear back from GeekReader," I said, sitting down in one of the four chairs Mrs. Davis had set out.

"It definitely can't hurt." Madeleine sat down next to me, leaving two empty chairs on the end.

CindeeRae sat down primly while March dropped down next to her, his arms still folded. "It was under control, Madeleine," he whispered so low I could hardly hear him.

Oblivious to the tension on our team, Mrs. Davis beamed in her striped jumpsuit and heels, looking boardroom ready. "I'm sure you already know that Dark Writer is about a disgruntled reporter who believes superheroes have taken advantage of their powers to rule over common citizens."

I nodded, although that was *all* we knew about Dark Writer. If she had any more information than that, we were already better off than we had been before. Madeleine leaned forward to catch March's eye, but he just scowled.

"I met a librarian at a conference last year who's a bit of a comic book expert." Mrs. Davis walked to the table and picked up the iPad, holding it so that we could all see. The screen displayed the cover of the first issue in the Dark Writer series. A thin kid with slicked-back hair and glasses was dwarfed in the dark shadow of a hulking beast with bony pincers on his back. The spindly appendages looked like they had just sprouted from his spine. "He's created a searchable database with just about every comic printed. It's not the first that's ever been made, but he tends to have more information than others I've seen. And rarer comics."

The description next to the cover read: "After Stan Wellerby's sister is killed in an incident involving a dark and nameless superhero, Stan considers what he can do, beyond writing useless newspaper articles, to uncover corruption and call for laws regulating superhero activity."

"There were five issues in the first and only volume of Dark Writer," Mrs. Davis said. "And I printed descriptions of each for you."

I shuffled through the five sheets and the stories' descriptions. The cover of the third issue had a squat figure wearing a black hoodie pulled over a red baseball cap. A bandanna, covering most of the person's face, was decorated with the picture of a skull. In bold block letters, the comic's title read, "Dark Writer: Quest for Vengeance."

March, studying his own handouts, read the third issue's summary aloud. "Ready to take on a more active role, Stan Wellerby becomes a vigilante, assuming the identity of Dark Writer. His quest? To end the lawless run of power-hungry superheroes."

"That's interesting," Madeleine said as she skimmed through the rest of the sheet.

"Why is it interesting?" March snapped.

"The reporter in the comic is anti-superhero," Madeleine said. "And superheroes are a big deal in comics. If our vandal hates comics like we think he does, it kinda makes sense that he would assume the identity of a superhero-hating vigilante."

"That is *very* interesting," Mrs. Davis agreed. "So you're researching the recent vandalism of Denver comic book stores?"

"Kinda," I said, unwilling to reveal too much about the case. I nodded at the magazine on the table. "Is that about Dark Writer, too?"

"In running my search for Dark Writer," Mrs. Davis began, "I came upon a short article in the *Denver Accolade*. Apparently Dark Writer was produced by a small Denver publisher called Relic Comics. They're not around anymore; in fact, they only produced Dark Writer and something called Calypso Robot. But I thought you might want to know about it anyway."

She distributed more copies to us and stood, brushing off her hands.

"Thank you, Mrs. Davis," I said. "That was super helpful."

"Yeah, thanks," March said begrudgingly. Although his arms were no longer folded across his chest, he still looked grouchy.

"Speaking of comics." Mrs. Davis nodded at Madeleine's shirt. "Did you know that Blood Eagle was a ritualized form of execution in Norse literature where the ribs were exposed to look like wings?"

"Yes!" Madeleine beamed, and even March's mouth twitched into a crooked smile. I shook my head and exchanged looks with CindeeRae, who was thinking the same thing I was: *Gross.* "The first edition of Blood Eagle was based on that, which is why his wings look like bones on my shirt. This is the very first Blood Eagle cover."

As if he couldn't resist, March barged into the conversation. "But the new publishers wanted to market to a bigger audience. So they changed Blood Eagle's image to make the ribs look like wings instead."

"Well done." Mrs. Davis nodded, pushing the glasses back to the bridge of her nose. "Sounds like you two are expert comic researchers yourselves."

I rolled my eyes as March sighed, a peaceful look settling on his face. All you had to do to sweet talk March Winters was mention comics, especially Blood Eagle. But even though Mrs. Davis had managed to soften him up, he still wouldn't look me in the eye when we parted for our different classrooms.

CHAPTER TWELVE

The theater was packed for the *Blood Eagle* opening, with pockets of kids we knew from Lincoln Elementary. As the film started, we were completely engrossed, our hands getting tangled in the popcorn bucket that CindeeRae held in the middle.

The movie was all about the comic's origin story, showing how Justin Wexler got his powers and then transformed into Blood Eagle at the end. Every now and then, a dramatic scene would draw a sigh or gasp from the audience, loud enough to drown out the movie's background music. But during the big battle scene, we all just stared, forgetting the popcorn and the soda and the people around us.

On-screen, Justin reached toward the sky, as if

preparing to hurl an imaginary boulder at his nemesis, Classynda Nightguard. But then his body slowly expanded with bulging muscles, and spiky appendages broke through his back, bony and jagged with sharp talons on the ends. Fully transformed, Blood Eagle flew toward a lunar eclipse and then dropped back down to earth, sending a shock wave that flattened the forest around him and killed Classynda.

The theater erupted in applause. "That guy definitely looks more like the original Blood Eagle," March said, not even trying to whisper. He pointed to the image on Madeleine's shirt for emphasis.

Even though the crowd had practically drowned March out, a big man in front of us turned around and shushed him.

"They don't look like wings at all," I said as the music swelled. With the jagged pincers curling from his back, this version of Blood Eagle felt so familiar.

Madeleine caught my eye, almost like she could hear my thoughts. "Blood Eagle looks a lot like . . ."

She trailed off as the big man in front turned around again and stared at us with buggy eyes. On the screen, Blood Eagle was gone and a bloody Justin Wexler stood in his place, hugging his best friend, Elaina, who had obviously just leveled up to his girlfriend.

"Sorry." Madeleine shrugged at the man and nodded toward the screen as end credits began to roll.

March stayed in his seat as the rest of us stood to leave. "Blood Eagle looks just like the creepy hero we saw on the cover of Dark Writer."

Madeleine shook her head. "But that doesn't make any sense. Blood Eagle and Dark Writer are completely different comics. They're not connected at all."

"But they look so much alike," I said. "That can't be a coincidence."

"There are all sorts of similarities in comic books." March finally followed us into the aisle. "Like Batman and Iron Man?"

"What?" CindeeRae interrupted. "They're not alike."

"They're both rich guys with fancy gadgets, not superpowers," Madeleine said. "But they don't *look* alike."

"You're right," March said, blowing out a sigh. "I've never seen two different comic book characters look *that* much alike."

"Maybe they're the same character," CindeeRae said, shaking the popcorn bucket so the kernels rattled around inside.

"What does that even mean?" I looked between the two comic book gurus, who shrugged. "And what does that have to do with *our* vandal?"

Before anyone could respond, we were jostled by the crowd from the lobby, and we walked silently out of the theater and into the chilly night.

Madeleine's mom picked us up in her SUV and drove us home, taking the long way down Federal Boulevard to March's and my neighborhood.

"That's a huge clue, guys!" Madeleine seemed to buzz with nervous energy. "Right?"

"The problem is," March said, "we don't know what it means. If it means anything at all. And taking the time to look into it might be a complete waste."

We sat in silence as the SUV cruised down a road lined with streetlights.

As we drove by the Super Pickle, March yelled, "Turn around!" Madeleine's mom jolted in the front seat.

"What?" Madeleine asked, turning to glance behind us. CindeeRae and I looked back, too, only seeing a steady stream of headlights.

"I saw something," March said. "At the Super Pickle."

Madeleine's mom turned right at the corner and parked alongside the road next to a church, looking at us through the rearview mirror. "What's going on?"

"Could we just check?" March asked. "Could we go back and make sure the Super Pickle's okay?" He looked pale under the interior car lights, his heavy brows casting dark shadows around his eyes.

"Please, Mom?" Madeleine asked.

Madeleine's mom sighed. "Only if someone tells me what, exactly, the Super Pickle is."

"It's a comic book store," Madeleine answered. "It belongs to March's uncle."

"Okay, then," Madeleine's mom said. "Just a quick look." She drove down the street and cut over one block to the comic book store. As soon as she pulled into the parking lot, March barged out of the vehicle, stumbling a bit before gaining his footing.

He gasped.

Slowly, the rest of us stepped from the car and walked to where March stood in front of a sweeping mural that covered the entire storefront.

There, sitting at a long table, sat a goofy-looking guy clutching a wad of cash in his hand. Atop the other end of the table sat a baby Blood Eagle, his face and body like the newer, redesigned character. Still, the bony wings curved over his back just like the image from Dark Writer's first cover. He was handing a wad of cash to the goofy-looking man. Just under the arc of the menacing rib-wings swirled the vandal's tag:

"Well," Madeleine said. "*This* Dark Writer definitely has a connection to Blood Eagle."

CHAPTER THIRTEEN

I was the last person to climb the ladder into March's family tree house, which he had turned into our investigation headquarters. When I got there, CindeeRae and Madeleine were gaping at the two walls March had covered with all our clues. A large Denver map hung from one wall with colored pushpins indicating the now four vandal hits. Red string connected each of the pins to Madeleine's pictures of the corresponding graffiti, which surrounded the map in a craggy border. On the other wall, March had hung newspaper articles, notes torn from his own detecting notebook, and the printouts Mrs. Davis had given us, ordered chronologically from top to bottom and left to right. Christmas tree lights hung from the ceiling, dangling by our heads, and a digital clock radio balanced in a small rectangular window. Only March Winters would want to keep track of time in a tree house.

"How long did this take you?" CindeeRae asked, almost tripping over a whiteboard with an agenda for today's meeting: *plan next operation.*

He shrugged. "Three days?"

"Wow." The ceiling was so low, Madeleine had to duck to check out the room. "This is a killer tree house, March."

We sat down on four overturned buckets covered with fleece blankets. "I couldn't get the folding chairs up the ladder," March apologized.

"We should have a party up here someday," Madeleine said, still distracted by the tree house. "My parents have a projector—we could watch movies and play video games."

"We need to focus on the case," March said. He was obviously still upset by the Super Pickle hit; his face looked drawn and tired, and his eyes were a little red. All of our hands were spotted with white paint from helping Owen cover up the graffiti earlier that afternoon, and March still had a splotch in his hair.

"Are you okay?" I asked. CindeeRae and Madeleine turned to stare at him, too.

"No," March admitted. "The Super Pickle hasn't been doing well for a while, and getting hit by the vandal isn't helping. Owen's trying to sell stuff online to pay the store's rent, so for now he's shutting down the Sorcery tournaments and our Defender games."

"No more Defender?" CindeeRae sounded a little whiny. "But it was just starting to get fun."

"Not helping," I whispered through my teeth.

"Sorry," CindeeRae said. "That's terrible, March."

"Let's just focus on the case," he said. "So we can catch this guy."

"But what do you think the mural means?" Madeleine asked. "That weird guy at the table taking money from the tiny Blood Eagle?"

"Maybe the vandal believes people who make comic books are greedy," I said.

"Or maybe," CindeeRae said, "the vandal believes *just* the people who made Blood Eagle are greedy."

"Phoenix Rising published Blood Eagle," Madeleine explained. "And I don't think anything else they made is popular."

"We can't get caught up in what it all means," March interrupted. "Some comics are popular and some aren't. You can't get mad at people for making money when something works."

"*We're* not," I said. "But the vandal might be."

"Yeah," Madeleine agreed. "It's a clue to his motivation."

March crossed his arms and looked out the window.

"Have there been any responses on GeekReader?" I asked, trying to change the subject.

"No," March said. "I mean, some people have talked about how rare Dark Writer is, and how they'd like to read a copy, too, but no one has actually seen the comic themselves."

We waited for him to go on. The Christmas lights flashed overhead, and Madeleine coughed into her elbow as I fiddled with the hem on my shirt.

When he didn't say anything, I finally broke the silence. "Remember how Mrs. Davis said Dark Writer was published somewhere in Denver?" I waved at the copy of the article she had found in the *Denver Accolade* tacked to the wall behind March's head. He looked over his shoulder, removed the copy from the wall, and nodded.

"Well," I said. "Maybe we could find the people who published it, and they could tell us Dark Writer's story. If we learn more about the comic, we might find more clues."

"They might even give us a copy of our own." Madeleine looked like she wanted to clap her hands.

March cleared his throat and said, "Do you *also* remember how Mrs. Davis said the publisher isn't around anymore?"

"That doesn't mean they're not really *around*

anymore," I said. "It just means they're not *publishing* anymore. If we could find the company—"

"Relic Comics," March interrupted, reading from Mrs. Davis's printout.

"We could find the people who can tell us more about Dark Writer's story," I finished.

"I was actually going to suggest that we start another mission." March tacked the sheet to the wall again and turned back around. "I think we've gone a little off track, focusing on what's motivating the vandal instead of who he actually is. The best operation for tracking him down would be to search for his practice site."

CindeeRae asked, "Where would we even start?"

"If you look at the map"—March left his bucket seat to hunch his way over to the opposite wall, waving at the group of pushpins crowding one section—"most of the hits are in West Highland. I say we start searching the neighborhoods surrounding the hits. I mean, there are tons of comic book stores all over Denver, but our vandal's staying in this area. I think it's because he lives somewhere close."

"But what happens when we find the practice site?" Madeleine asked. "We're still no closer to finding our vandal."

"Then we perform surveillance," March said, like it was the most logical plan in the universe. "We take turns watching the practice site until our vandal shows up. And when he does, we call the police and, voilà, case solved."

"We take turns watching the site?" CindeeRae asked, and March nodded. "Like, late at night when no one is around, and we're supposed to be in bed?"

He shrugged. "It's a sure way to catch our vandal."

"But what about finding someone who knows the Dark Writer story?" I asked, my voice louder than I'd intended. "I mean, that was *your* plan in the first place—learn more about the Dark Writer story so we can figure out what our vandal is planning to do next."

CindeeRae sat up straighter, ready to smooth things over. "Maybe we can do both."

"Why should we do both?" March harrumphed like an old man and sat back on his bucket. "One plan catches the guy."

"If you're okay *performing surveillance* until we're grandparents," Madeleine said.

"We need to figure out *why* he's doing this." I used my most soothing voice. "If we're patient, like you said, we'll figure out what he wants, and *then* we can catch him."

"Or," March said, "we're patient and we catch the guy. We skip a whole step with my plan."

"Guys!" CindeeRae stood up abruptly and accidentally slammed her head on the ceiling. She cried out and dropped to the floor, cradling her head in her hands.

"Are you okay?" Madeleine asked, and then looked back at me with wide eyes.

The three of us crouched over her. She moaned, and I realized she was saying something.

"Staff sighting?" I asked.

"Stand mighty," Madeleine said.

"Stop fighting," March yelled. "She's asking us to stop fighting."

"Oh," I said.

As CindeeRae sat up, I realized that at least March's plan had us doing something. He *was* acting lead investigator, and maybe CindeeRae was right: We could do both. Madeleine and I could perform our own operations on the side.

As long as March never found out.

CHAPTER FOURTEEN

I sprawled out on the living room rug and began scrolling through Madeleine's pictures on my SleuthPad. It was late, and Genki nosed my ribs, ready to head up to bed. Mom and Dad were having a serious conversation in their room, and even though they had shut their door, I could still hear their sharp voices snapping back and forth. I had never heard my parents fight before, and it left me feeling lost, like the walls and the floors of my own home were suddenly unfamiliar.

Genki could hear, too, and a whimper squeaked from somewhere in his throat. Eventually, he stopped whining and turned in about ten circles before he finally flopped down next to me, his breathing deep and soothing. I curled myself around him and tried to focus on Madeleine's pictures.

After the Super Pickle hit, I had asked her to send them to me so I could add the collection to my case files. I flicked through picture after picture. Not only had the vandal's murals gotten better and better, but the colors in Madeleine's photographs were bright and clear, and most of the angles were unusual and interesting. Even though she was taking them for our records, Madeleine and the vandal's combined work looked like something you could hang in a museum.

"What is that?"

I jumped at the sound of Baa-chan's voice behind me. At first I thought she was talking about Mom and Dad's argument, but then I realized she was looking at my SleuthPad. "Pictures of graffiti," I answered.

I expected Baa-chan to scoff at the images and send me to my room. Instead she said, "Sugoi ne!" and sat down on the couch to get a better look.

"I know!" I responded, happy to hear that someone else was as impressed by our vandal as I was. I got up and sat next to Baa-chan on the couch, opening a picture of the vandal's mural on Comic Warehouse. She took the SleuthPad from me and studied the painting. Genki sat at Baa-chan's feet, watching her like she had doggie treats in her pockets. She scrolled through all the pictures, enlarging some with her fingers to see details.

When she was done, she leaned back into the couch and said, "I knew a street artist once."

"What?!" I gawked at her. "When? How? Why?"

"After high school, I only wanted to become an artist. I studied for some years, but my parents wanted other things. They were happy for me to marry Jii-chan and move to America for graduate school. I was happy, too, because I could still study art."

"I didn't know you went to art school." I hadn't ever thought of what Baa-chan was like when she was younger. Imagining her studying to become an artist was like realizing she had wings or something.

"I only took a few classes at North Seattle University before I became pregnant with your mother," she said. "But I loved it there and met so many amazing artists."

"And?" I was anxious for her to get to the street artist part of her story.

"I met a young man who told me his secret." She smiled to herself before continuing, her eyes glassy with the memory. "We sat next to each other in a sculpture class, and he talked and talked and talked and talked. By midterm, we were good friends, and by at the end of the semester he told me he was a street artist named Babo. No one else knew, but you could tell he was proud."

"He told you before he told anyone else?" Goose bumps spread across my arms.

"That's what he said." Baa-chan looked proud, too. "After Yumi was born I would push her stroller for hours as we walked through the city, looking for Babo's work. I took a picture every time I found something; I have a thick envelope of photographs at home. Someday I'll show you."

When I was seven, we had visited my grandparents shortly after they had moved back to Japan. Baa-chan had pulled a box from her bedroom cabinet full of envelopes loaded with pictures. Each was labeled with a year or an event, like *Yumi's high school graduation* or *Summer vacation 1995*. Baa-chan had handed me about ten envelopes to go through, and I pored over the pictures of my mother when she was my age. I could only imagine an envelope full of *Babo the street artist*. Or *North Seattle University*.

"What about *your* artwork?" I asked.

"I haven't made anything in years." She looked at the ceiling. This dreamy grandma was my favorite. "I miss it, though."

I stayed next to her, enjoying the warmth of her side while I scrolled through the rest of Madeleine's pictures. When we reached the end, she said, "It's getting late. You better go to bed."

I stood, clutching the SleuthPad to my chest. Genki stretched before trotting to the stairs. Mom and Dad's room had gone silent, and I wondered if that was a good thing or a bad thing.

"I know," Baa-chan said, stopping me before I could leave. "What if I taught you some shodō?"

I remembered the long sheets of paper back at Baa-chan's house, filled with kanji she had painted herself. The Japanese characters were like pictures, with sweeping lines that often looked like the words they stood for. Mom had once taught me how to write *mountain*: 山, *river*: 川, and *tree*: 木. I had always thought it would be fun to create sentences made of pictures instead of letters.

"That sounds great," I said, and even though I meant it, my smile faded as I turned back toward the stairs.

"Kazu-chan," she said, and her tone stopped me in my tracks. "Everything will be fine."

I turned back to her, feeling like she had just X-ray visioned my heart. "Thanks, Baa-chan," I said, wanting to believe her.

"O-yasumi-nasai."

"Good night," I answered, wishing I could stay downstairs, cozy with Baa-chan, for just a little bit longer.

CHAPTER FIFTEEN

After my parents' fight on Saturday night, I spent most of Sunday in my room, investigating Mom's case.

Using my SleuthPad, I searched nervous system disorders and made a list of all the diseases she might have: Bell's palsy, epilepsy, Parkinson's disease, Guillain-Barré syndrome, multiple sclerosis, neurofibromatosis.

Each sickness seemed to have more syllables than the last, and they stacked like bricks on my chest. None of those things sounded easy to heal, but all of them included fatigue as a symptom. This could explain why Mom had spent so much time in bed lately and needed Baa-chan's help around the house.

Genki seemed to sense how uneasy the case was making me and tried to burrow his nose into my armpit, pushing me away from my SleuthPad. I surrendered, grateful for the break, and pressed my forehead against his until we were breathing in sync. This was the first time a case had made me feel this anxious, and I hoped that solving it would unclench my heart.

But I had to do more than guess Mom's sickness. Maybe I could trick Dr. Bassi's office into telling me her diagnosis. Brainstorming a new mission, I jotted notes in my SleuthPad to follow the next time I worked on the case. Just as I powered down and settled into the Sunday comics, Baa-chan called my name up the stairs.

I cracked my door open to yell back, "Yes, Baa-chan?"

"Please come."

I heard a rustling noise in the dining room, and I followed the sound until I found her standing at the table over a narrow sheet of paper held down with a weighted bar. A thick paintbrush balanced across an ink dish.

"Shodō shiyō ka?" Baa-chan asked, dipping the brush into the dish and holding it over the paper.

"What's shodō?" I asked, pulling out a chair next to her and sitting down to watch.

"No, no, no!" she said before I could get comfortable. "You're going to do it yourself."

She turned to the paper and began sweeping the

page, the brush moving quickly at first, leaving short points in its wake. Then she slowed, and the marks became thicker, the final downstroke flicking up at the very end before she lifted the paintbrush from the page: 火. It was like watching a dance. "Fire?" I could almost see the logs of a campfire, sparks leaping to the sky.

"Yes, *fire!*" she said.

"Mom taught me a bunch of kanji when I was little, but I never painted them."

"Shodō is Japanese calligraphy," she said, and while I watched, she swept the page to make *water*: 水. "When we do shodō, we write the characters—or the kanji—like that."

"It looks hard."

"A little." She held out a paintbrush like it was a magic wand. "But you'll get better with practice."

I took the brush from her and dipped it into the ink tray. Baa-chan held her own brush over the *water* kanji and showed me the strokes. "One, two, three, four."

I copied her, trying to be as swoopy as she had been. It looked like a sloppy, double-sided *K*.

"See?" she said. "Yoku dekita." *You did well.* I gave her a look that was all eyebrows.

I practiced *water* again before trying *fire.* As I focused on the brushstrokes, the knot in my chest loosened a little, and my breathing wasn't so achy.

Baa-chan worked by my side, removing her used sheet of paper and replacing it with a clean one. "I came here to help your mother, but I'm starting to worry more about you."

I concentrated on filling my sheet of paper with another *fire* kanji as I answered, "I'm fine."

Baa-chan painted the kanji for *person* while I got a clean sheet of paper. I focused on the easier, two-stroke character, hoping Baa-chan wouldn't ask me any more questions.

"Your mother is in pain, and it appears her pain is a little contagious," she said. "Pain is uncomfortable, but it isn't always bad. And sometimes we must feel the pain before we can feel better. That goes for your mother, and for you, too."

Why would feeling pain help me feel better? That made no sense. But then I thought about the pain that had been twisting in my chest all day today. A pain that had started to unravel as I painted kanji.

"But why does she stay in her room so much?" I asked.

"She'll return to herself after she learns to live with this particular pain," Baa-chan said, which did not answer my question at all. She painted another stroke.

"What pain?" I pressed.

She stopped painting and met my gaze. "She'll tell you when she's ready."

I bit my lip in frustration and painted the *person* kanji. 人. At first it looked like someone taking big steps. And then it looked like someone splitting in half. I wondered if both could be true of someone at the same time.

CHAPTER SIXTEEN

The next morning, I woke up earlier than usual and rushed through the paper route so I could meet March on the corner of Summer Glen and Colonial to start the practice-site search.

Tired from the route, I huffed my way over to our meeting spot, two extra newspapers rolling around in my basket next to my SleuthPad. March stood on the corner by the stop sign, a map of Denver spread open on the handlebars, which he was highlighting meticulously. He wore a dark ski mask and a green puffer jacket.

I skidded to a stop next to him and said, "You don't look suspicious at all." I had meant it as a joke, but it came out sounding snarky and mean. Or maybe the reason it sounded bad was because our last meeting had ended so terribly.

March jumped at my voice and pulled the mask up so I could see his face. "It's still a little nippy."

Genki tugged on his leash and sniffed at March.

I grabbed the mask from March's head and tossed it into my basket. "Where are we starting?"

He studied the map again before passing it to me, pointing at the neon-green square he'd outlined. "Comic Warehouse is by Lincoln Park. There are some alleys and buildings we can check out. It's a little farther away, but if we head over now, we'll still have time to get ready for school."

"Okay." I shrugged. "I'll follow you."

March folded the map and shoved it into his back pocket before standing on his pedals and wobbling ahead of me. The old Sorcery cards on his spokes clicked as we rode. We started slowly, cycling down Speer Boulevard and cutting down Clay Street to avoid the freeway.

While we weren't meddling in the case like Detective Hawthorne had cautioned us, we had still crossed Federal Boulevard, which both our parents had said was out of bounds. Usually this would freak March out, but he passed Mile High Stadium and rode under the overpass like we did this every day. I nodded my head, impressed. It's amazing how leadership responsibilities can change a person.

Just as we were about to cross the South Platte River, we saw a cluster of fenced lots with big trucks parked inside, warehouses, smokestacks, and a power plant. I had to admit, this was a good choice. It was isolated without much traffic. A street artist could easily practice a mural on the backside of any of these buildings without being seen.

March looked over his shoulder, and I could tell he was thinking the same thing. "We're only a few blocks away from Lincoln Park," he called. "Should we start here?"

I nodded and slowed down. Genki tugged on the leash, trying to pull me back. Good thing my guard dog couldn't talk, because he looked like he was ready to call my parents and rat me out.

I felt a flutter in my chest as we turned onto a narrow road and crossed the railroad tracks. Usually *I* was the fearless member on our team, ready to plow forward without wondering whether our plans were safe or smart. But March and I seemed to have switched roles, and suddenly I was the one worrying what might happen to us out here in the middle of nowhere. Maybe it was because I knew Mom's mystery illness prevented her from fretting over my every move.

Before Mom got sick, she had the keenest observations skills in the house; I inherited my master detecting talents from her. Without her super snooping to ensure I didn't do anything dangerous or break any rules, no one would even miss me if I got lost in the dark alleys of downtown Denver for a few hours. She would probably be in her room until lunch, and Dad would leave for work before I even got back. The only one to notice me was Baa-chan, who might complain if I missed the bus. *Right?* I wondered to myself. Although, after last night, it seemed Baa-chan cared more than I had thought.

Aside from a couple of random tags, we couldn't see anything. We turned back onto 13th and made our way toward Lincoln Park, veering onto cross streets and searching between buildings and behind dumpsters for a trace of our vandal.

After about twenty minutes, March braked and pulled the map from his back pocket. "We better head back before anyone notices we're gone." This time he pulled a Sharpie from his puffer jacket and crossed out all the streets we had just searched. "So we know where we've been." March Winters, techie guru and search strategist extraordinaire.

"Good job!" I said. Genki lay down on the sidewalk next to me, tired of waiting.

"Really?" March looked up with a half smile.

I nodded. Best friends since before kindergarten, March and I had experienced our fair share of fights, but this time felt more personal. Things seemed to be changing between us, and I didn't like it.

"I have some good news." He pushed both the folded map and the Sharpie back into his jacket pocket. "Someone responded on GeekReader late last night."

"Did they post pictures from the comic?" I couldn't believe he hadn't said anything earlier.

"No," he said, grabbing the ski mask from my basket and pulling it back over his face. "But she'd heard someone was planning to sell a complete Dark Writer set at the Denver ComiCanon next month."

You couldn't be best friends with the biggest comic book fan on the planet and not know what ComiCanon was. It was like an expert-level Halloween party where people gathered, in costume, as their favorite characters from books, video games, movies, or television shows. There were panel discussions about Star Wars and Gravity Falls, group pictures of different fandoms, geeky products sold at vendor booths, and, of course, comic books everywhere. March had been with his family twice before, and I loved scrolling through all the pictures they had taken. When March died, he wouldn't go to heaven; he would go to ComiCanon.

"That's cool," I said. "But how will *we* see it?"

"We'll go to ComiCanon," he said matter-of-factly through the ski mask.

"Okay," I said. "But how will we pay for it?" I tried to imagine how much the ultra-rare Dark Writer comic set would cost, not to mention ComiCanon tickets.

"A fund-raiser?" he said. "I'm not sure yet, but you'll help me figure it out. Like you always do."

He was making amends, and for some reason it made me feel glum. "Not *always*." The sharp words stuck in my throat.

"Is everything okay?" March asked, cocking his head to study me.

"Of course!" I lied. "If we have a fund-raiser, you *have* to wear the weenie costume."

His younger brother, Mason, had spent all his allowance on a hot-dog costume he discovered at a thrift store last summer, and March had borrowed it when we were looking for ways to get more traffic to our lemonade stand. It was way too small and gave March a wedgie. Not only did it get people's attention, but it made me laugh so hard, my stomach muscles ached for a week.

March smirked. "That doesn't seem fair."

"Hey," I said, turning my bike around and pointing it homeward. "If it helps us solve the case . . ."

"All right," he said, trying to tame his smile. "If it helps us solve the case."

Genki tugged on the leash, whimpering again at the unfamiliar surroundings.

"Lead the way," March called from behind me, and I took off, pedaling fast to chase out the anxiety that pushed on my chest at the thought of my other unsolved case.

CHAPTER SEVENTEEN

"Let's get ice cream!" Dad said as he finished loading the dishwasher in the kitchen that night. Mom sat at the bar, leaning over the counter on her elbows while Baa-chan put the leftovers in plastic containers.

We always joked that Chocolate Chunk flowed through Mom's veins. She had stacked at least twenty pints in the garage freezer, bought on double-coupon day during a flash sale, and hid a couple in the freezer drawer in the kitchen where she thought I couldn't find them. Her face perked up at Dad's suggestion, and I knew it was a deal.

I was rushing to wipe down the dining room table when Mom said, "Bring me back a single cup?"

I looked from her to Dad. "Or," I said, "we can all go through the Frosty Scoop drive-thru and bring it back home."

Dad smiled at Mom. "The drive would do you good."

Mom looked doubtful. But Baa-chan was on our side. She smiled at Mom and said, "Go, Yumi-chan. It won't be long."

"I don't know," Mom said, but I walked toward the front door like I hadn't heard her.

"Aren't you coming, too, Baa-chan?" I asked, my heart thrumming as Mom stood and followed me.

"I have chores to do." She winked at me for the first time in my life. "But I'll take rainbow sherbet in a cone."

Dad rested his hand on Mom's lower back, guiding her out the door and toward the car.

As we drove, Mom stared out the window and hummed one of her favorite Smashing Pumpkins songs called "Today." It had always sounded like a happy song to me and hearing her hum it made me happy, too. I blurted, "The team decided to raise money for ComiCanon tickets, and I was wondering if we could have a car wash and bake sale at our house." After our search that morning, March had sent out a team text, and everyone agreed to an operation at the geeky convention. Whether or not we would be able to read all five Dark Writer issues while we were there—without paying for them—was still questionable.

Mom stopped humming, and it felt like I had just told a fart joke in church. When no one said anything, I rambled on, "We're closest to Federal Boulevard and could probably get a lot of traffic. We'd do all the work, even the baking, and you wouldn't even have to come outside."

Mom began to nod, but Dad spoke before she could say anything. "Bug, I think it's a great idea for earning money, but now isn't the best time for doing something like that at our house."

I slumped in my seat, frustrated that Dad hadn't even given Mom the chance to respond. I knew he was only trying to prevent her from feeling stressed, but if going on a drive for ice cream was good for her, why wouldn't it also help to have a fund-raiser at our house? I turned to the window and watched the scenery go by as Mom continued to hum.

When Dad pulled into the Frosty Scoop's drive-thru lane, Mom stopped humming and turned around in her seat to look at me. "I could probably make some snickerdoodles for the bake sale. Maybe even a batch of cupcakes?"

We could turn around and go back home right then and there, and I wouldn't even miss the ice cream one bit; that's how happy I felt. Could something as simple as a drive for Chocolate Chunk cure Mom of her bedroom sickness?

"And maybe Baa-chan would like to make a Japanese treat," she added.

"Anpan!" I said, excited to hear Mom planning with me.

"Are you sure?" Mom asked. "I mean, anko is kind of an acquired taste."

Anpan was a sweet Japanese bun filled with anko, a yummy red-bean paste. Every time Mom took me to Tokyo Premium Bakery, I ordered one anpan to eat there, and one melon pan for later.

"Are you kidding?" I said, hope floating in my chest like a balloon. "Anpan is delicious!"

I beamed the whole way home, holding Baa-chan's cone in one hand and my own bubble-gum cone in the other, not even noticing the melted ice cream dripping down my fingers until we pulled into the driveway.

• • •

That whole next day at school, I planned my phone call with Dr. Bassi. If I was going to solve this case, I needed to go directly to the source of information: Mom's neurologist. I jotted down a bunch of questions I thought would get them to share her diagnosis with me, but I knew I would have to pretend to be her if I wanted them to tell me the truth. In order for this mission to be successful, I would have to use Mom's smartphone to download a voice-changing app that would help me sound old enough to be my own mother. Easy peasy.

By the time I got home, my stomach churned with excitement and nerves. The kitchen was empty, but there was something sweet baking in the oven. I opened the oven door to see a cookie sheet filled with golden rolls, and I took in a deep breath to savor the smell of anpan.

"Looks delicious, doesn't it?" Baa-chan's voice boomed behind me, and I jumped, releasing the oven door so that it slammed shut.

"Baa-chan, you scared me!"

She chuckled softly, and then passed me a little cup filled with sesame seeds. Fitting her hands with oven mitts, she opened the oven again, pulled out the cookie sheet, and set the rolls on the counter. "I'll brush each bun with egg yolk, and you sprinkle them with sesame seeds."

We worked silently as Baa-chan used what looked like a paintbrush to glaze the top of each bun with egg yolk. I followed her, dusting the rolls with the tiny, pale seeds.

"Perfect!" she said. "Would you like to try one?"

My tongue tickled at the idea of some fresh, warm anpan, but I knew I had to keep working on my mission. "Mom loves anpan," I said, and it wasn't even a lie. "Can I take her some, too?"

Baa-chan was already walking to the cabinet to pull

out two small plates, as if she had read my mind. "That's a wonderful idea," she said. "But don't tire her. After yesterday's outing she's feeling a little worn out."

Her words stung. Did she blame me for getting ice cream last night? I thought we all agreed that ice-cream outings made for a logical nightly prescription in Mom's recovery.

I shook the criticism away and continued on my mission, balancing a plate in each hand as I went up to Mom's room, Genki padding behind me.

Luckily, the door wasn't latched closed, and I could push it open with my hip. Mom was propped up on the pillows and tucked under the covers, staring straight ahead. For a second, I wanted to back out of the room, uneasy at her intense, directionless gaze.

"Mom?"

It was like she was hearing my voice from far away. She looked around the room and sighed when she saw me. "Oh, Kazu. I got caught up in a daydream. I didn't see you there."

"Baa-chan made anpan." I held out the plates, unsure what else to say.

Mom nodded at the head of her bed, and I sat down, handing her one perfect bun, toasted to a honey-golden crisp. She pulled it into two pieces, exposing the red anko center and a puff cloud of steam. "Oh, it's fresh from the oven!"

I took a dainty bite from the end of mine, intending to savor my anpan as long as possible.

"She wasn't sure how they'd cook at this elevation." Mom spoke around her first bite. "So she's practicing before the bake sale."

"They seem perfect to me." As I reached the sweet center, I couldn't resist taking a big bite. An involuntary smile stretched across my face. "They're so good!"

Mom laughed. "Don't talk with your mouth full."

We ate our treats in silence, and when Mom finished, she handed me the plate. "I can't believe I ate the whole thing."

I took it from her, spying her cell phone on the nightstand. "Can I borrow your phone to call March?" I asked, keeping my voice as even as possible.

"Where's the emergency phone?" Mom pierced me with her gaze, and I scrambled to think of a reason I would need her smartphone instead. Then she shrugged. "Oh, go ahead. Just return it when you're done."

"Thanks!" I stood and pocketed the phone. "I'll bring it back in a minute."

I shoved the second half of the anpan in my mouth and walked to the door.

"Slow down," Mom said. "You're going to choke yourself!"

My cheeks were full, so I couldn't answer, but I gave her a thumbs-up instead.

CHAPTER EIGHTEEN

I paced my room a few times before I finally got the nerve to call Dr. Bassi's office. Avoiding the cyborg, alien, and chipmunk options, I selected old lady on the voice-changing app and punched in the number. Genki watched me from his blanket nest on my bed.

"Denver Neurological Center," a woman said in a tight voice. "How can I help you?"

"I'm calling for Dr. Bassi," I said. The old-lady option on the app was the closest I could find to a grown-up voice. It had sounded a little silly when I tested it, but I thought it would work as long as the person I spoke to didn't actually know Mom.

"Did you want to schedule an appointment or speak with the nurse?"

"Um, I just need to talk to somebody about . . . my condition."

"I'll transfer you to the nurse."

Classical music played while I waited, and my breath shuddered as I tried to calm myself down. Dr. Bassi's nurse must remember Mom, especially if she'd been visiting the office every month. This old-lady voice would be a dead giveaway, and I'd be back where I started with hardly any clues.

"Denise Barnes." The nurse's voice was deep and soothing. "How can I help you?"

I cleared my throat, and then worried about what it sounded like through the app. "This is Yumi Jones. And I've been struggling with . . . my symptoms and was wondering if there was something I could do at home without coming into the office."

"Which symptoms are you struggling with most?" she asked.

This was the tricky part: getting the nurse to reveal Mom's diagnosis. My heart was beating so hard I could feel my pulse echoing in my eardrum. "Fatigue, mostly. Lethargy, apathy." I had looked a few words up in the thesaurus so I could sound more grown-up.

"Just a second," she said. "Let me open your file." I wondered if that was code for trace the call so they could come and arrest me for impersonating my mother.

The seconds ticked away, feeling like hours, and

when she returned, her voice was slow and curious. "Have the migraines returned?"

I knew migraines were really bad headaches only because when I was in the third grade, Mom got them so bad she had to see a specialist for help. The information snapped together like puzzle pieces in my mind. Dr. Bassi wasn't the person Mom had been seeing for the past four months. She had been the specialist Mom visited two years ago to help her migraines go away. For a minute, I thought about hanging up, but then I realized she might call Mom back to see why they had been disconnected.

"Actually, I accidentally called the wrong doctor," I said. "I'm sorry to bother you."

"Mrs. Jones," Nurse Denise said, her voice swollen with concern, "please let us know if there's anything we can do to help."

"Definitely," I said, ending the call.

Genki jumped from the bed to follow me as I paced the room a couple more times. Relief washed over me as I thought about all those multisyllabic neurological diseases I had been researching, which I now knew Mom didn't have. But then the familiar anxiety clenched round my heart again.

I was back at square one, with no clues. I needed a new lead, and I had no idea where to look for it. What kind of detective can't even help her own mother?

• • •

After dinner on Friday night, Mom and Dad disappeared into their room while Baa-chan retreated to the window seat to knit. She had been working on something since she'd come, but I had never been interested enough to ask her about it. With nothing else to do, I decided to sit down and watch her, and maybe try to extract information she might have about Mom's condition.

"What are you making?" I asked, studying the two pieces of paper that lay between us: a sheet with a color code for temperatures and another with a list of local daily averages for the last two weeks.

"A temperature scarf," Baa-chan said. She explained that she had started knitting in January at the suggestion of one of her old Seattle friends, when she was still in Japan. The navy, royal, and light blues were for colder temperatures, while greens and yellows represented warmer, springier temperatures.

I studied the thick scarf that hung in Baa-chan's lap, shaking back and forth as she worked, like a dancing puppet ruled by the clicking needles. A thick border of deep blue lined the bottom. But as the rows progressed, the blues alternated with dark green. Then lime, olive, and at last bright yellow, which would make up the majority of the past week. Looking at the scarf, you couldn't even tell when Baa-chan had left Japan for Colorado.

"I didn't know Wednesday and Thursday were so cold," I said as I studied the sheet. Wednesday and Thursday had been difficult days for Mom, too, and I wondered what a blanket of someone's moods might look like. It seemed our family had been smothered by too many blue days stacked together.

"Soon it will only be yellow," Baa-chan said, her knitting needles clicking together without pause. "If I stay long enough, I might be able to add magenta. We rarely get magenta days in Nagano."

July and August could get especially hot in Denver; we'd sometimes have a few days in a row where the temperature would go over 100 degrees. But that was months away. Would Baa-chan really need to stay that long to help Mom get better?

I watched her finish one row and start on the next before I asked, "Who's it for?"

"In the beginning," Baa-chan said, "it was a gift for someone special to me, someone that I hadn't met yet. But circumstances changed, and I've decided to give it to O-jizō-sama instead."

I cocked my head at her, confused. "You're giving a scarf to a lawn ornament?"

"He's more than that," Baa-chan said. "But it's also symbolic. The person I was planning to give it to isn't here anymore, and I'll give it to O-jizō-sama in hopes that he'll carry that person to the afterlife."

It sounded like a riddle. Who was special to Baa-chan that she hadn't yet met and had died before she could give them this scarf? My mind squished around the crazy conditions of this strange relationship, and I wanted to come right out and ask who she was talking about. But it felt like this was all she was willing to tell me right now. Then I remembered my mission and decided I couldn't get distracted by silly riddles. I needed to search for more clues about Mom.

"Do you know which doctor Mom was seeing when she got sick?" I thought the most direct question was the best. Since Mom hadn't kept the doctor's number in her phone, maybe Baa-chan could at least tell me who it was.

The needles stopped clicking, and Baa-chan rested her hands in her lap before turning to meet my eyes. "You're worried about your mother," she said. "But she's not sick in that way. Her heart is sick."

"But why?" I asked, the question spilling from my mouth.

Baa-chan picked up the needles and started knitting again, only this time the clicks were irregular, hesitant. "Kazu-chan, I would tell you if I thought it was my place. But it's not. You need to ask your parents." Her voice was gentle but sure, unwavering, and solid.

But I had already tried asking Dad, and he wouldn't tell me. And now Baa-chan wouldn't tell me either, although I could tell she wanted me to know. She trusted I could handle it. Why didn't my parents?

"It'll be okay," Baa-chan assured me. "It may take time, but it'll be okay."

The heavy weight settled back onto my chest, and I blinked away the frustration.

I stayed on the bench for a while, leaning into Baa-chan as I watched her work. Maybe it wouldn't be so bad if she stayed for magenta days.

CHAPTER NINETEEN

Even though it wasn't warm enough for shorts, CindeeRae, Madeleine, and I wore them anyway for our car wash, the cool air and hose water raising goose bumps on our legs as we worked. March had volunteered to stand on the corner of Federal Boulevard and Viking Road in the weenie costume, trying to lure customers to Madeleine's posh block on Saint Anthony while bopping around and waving a sign.

We washed cars in their circular driveway, a line that had been backed up since we started at ten that morning. Most of them were shiny vehicles from Madeleine's neighborhood, probably her parents' fancy friends.

Madeleine's mom had set up a long craft table that was crowded with baked goods, and she stood by the driveway taking money for car washes and treats as customers drove through. Even though she was really a lawyer, she was a natural saleswoman, her voice hoarse from calling out to drivers about all the sweets they needed in their lives.

"Good morning, Kathleen," she yelled as a woman in a blue minivan pulled into our wash zone. "I know you have a big family that could use some cookies, brownies, cinnamon rolls, or this authentic Japanese treat, anpan." I rolled my eyes as she held up one of Baa-chan's plates, covered with the shiny, golden buns.

While Mom had been excited about participating last week, she'd apparently lost her enthusiasm yesterday. I tried to exhale the disappointment from my chest, but it stayed put, crowding my insides like a dark fog. Baa-chan had tried making up for it by baking Mom's snickerdoodles anyway, in addition to the anpan she had practiced last week, which I was hoping wouldn't sell so Mom and I could eat the leftovers later. But there were only two plates left, and apparently Kathleen, the woman in the blue minivan, needed both of them for her family, as well as a half-dozen cinnamon rolls March's mom had made.

We scrubbed the minivan, using a system Madeleine had perfected over the past hour, directing us like one of those air traffic controllers but without the light-up wands. Madeleine got the front, CindeeRae worked on the driver's side, and I cleaned the passenger's side. Soon CindeeRae and I made our way to the back, while Madeleine began hosing down the front, a cool mist sprinkling down on us. We all wiped off the excess water with rags that Madeleine's dad kept bringing out in laundry baskets heaped high and still warm.

"Good job!" Madeleine yelled, cheering us on.

Kathleen pulled through, and a new silver Jeep took the minivan's place just as March returned to help. His face was red and sweaty. "Watch this," he yelled from the street as we waited for Madeleine's mom to take the driver's money. March reenacted his hot-dog dance for us, scissoring his feet at the end and pumping the sign back and forth from his chest. I grinned. No wonder our car wash was so popular.

We cleaned together until the crisp morning turned hot, the sun burning high above us. Madeleine started hosing us all down in between cars, and we sloshed through our work, wet as our sponges. I was so busy imagining all the money we were earning for ComiCanon tickets that I didn't notice Catelyn Monson and Elesha Williams riding their bikes, swerving up and down the block, until Madeleine asked if she could trade me places.

I stared at her. Was this the same Madeleine Brown kids had been afraid of just last year? The girl who could silence an entire lunchroom table with a glare?

"Please?" she asked, and I nodded, taking my post at the hood of the next car.

Catelyn dropped her bike to the curb in front of Madeleine's house and flounced over in her purple soccer uniform. Her cleats clicked on the driveway until she stopped next to me, eyeing our work with her hands on her hips. Elesha rode onto the sidewalk before she stopped and pushed down her kickstand, tentatively approaching our group in a matching uniform.

"Catelyn!" Madeleine's mom crooned. "It's been a while since we've seen you. How are you doing?"

Catelyn smiled sweetly. "I'm doing fine, Mrs. Brown." She swept her arm toward Elesha like a game-show host and said, "This is my new friend, Elesha. She's on *our* soccer team." She said *our* like it was a puppy Madeleine had abandoned.

"Nice to meet you, Elesha," Madeleine's mom said, unwrapping a plate of chocolate chip cookies and holding it out to them. "I'm sure you'll both have a great season without Madeleine. She's enjoying a break from sports right now."

I looked back at Madeleine and tried to read her expression. It seemed everyone at Lincoln Elementary knew she had quit soccer, but no one could say why. She scrubbed madly at the car's back door, her face blank. March worked next to her, his red hot-dog cap flapping up and down as he bobbed his head to a song only he could hear. Catelyn and Elesha each took a cookie, which Catelyn ate in two bites and Elesha began to nibble.

Madeleine's mom grabbed a cookie for herself and set the plate back on the table. "Nice to see you, girls," she said. "But I better get back to work."

We continued in silence, wiping down the car with rags. When Madeleine's mom had moved away, Catelyn turned to us and hissed, "What are you weirdos doing?"

My stomach tightened at her tone, the way *weirdos* cut into me like a swearword. Madeleine must have felt the same way, because her head snapped up and she met Catelyn's eyes.

"Helllllllooo!" Catelyn called. "Does anyone hear me?"

"We hear you!" I said, matching Catelyn's pose: hands on my hips, the sponge leaking sudsy water down my leg. "We're raising money."

"What for?" she asked. "You guys aren't part of any group or club."

"We are, too," CindeeRae called from where she rubbed the next car's hubcaps. She looked from Catelyn to Madeleine and back again, and added, her voice thick with sass, "We're the most important group—a group of friends. Do you know what that is?"

I peeked at Madeleine, who smiled crookedly.

Catelyn huffed and turned to go. Elesha stayed

behind, still nibbling on her cookie. Picking her bike up from the curb, Catelyn called out, "Madeleine, why are you being such a freak?"

Madeleine didn't answer, but the question shook March from his daze, and his face pinched into a scowl. "What is it with you people?" he asked. "It's like you don't want anyone else to be happy." The statement seemed especially poignant coming from a boy dressed as a weenie.

Catelyn rolled her eyes and barked at Elesha to follow. The new girl brushed the cookie crumbs from her hands and whispered, "Sorry," before jogging after Catelyn with her bike at her side, the pedals hitting the kickstand with a *clack, clack, clack*.

Once they were out of sight, we just looked at one another. I noticed Madeleine's mom had returned to the wash zone.

"I never liked that girl in the first place," she muttered. Then she turned and cooed to our next customer, "Levi, I know you want to save me from these snickerdoodles!"

CHAPTER TWENTY

Everyone on our team was suddenly very interested in helping with my paper route—at least that's what they were telling their parents. After I finished the route on Sunday, CindeeRae and Madeleine joined March, Genki, and me in canvassing Denver for our vandal's practice site. Last week March and I had finished searching the area around Comic Warehouse where our vandal had last hit. Today we were searching the opposite end of West Highland.

March and I usually rode our bikes in silence, but today CindeeRae grilled Madeleine nonstop:

Why is Catelyn mad at you?

Why aren't you playing soccer?

Do you talk to her anymore?

Who chooses uniform colors? Because purple is weird.

How long have you guys been friends anyway? And did you take mean classes together or something?

The sun glowed orange at the horizon, and the wind carried Madeleine's short responses to where March and I rode in front.

Because I don't play soccer anymore.

I just didn't want to.

Not really.

What's wrong with purple?

Since first grade.

What?

When I peeked behind me every now and then, I could see Madeleine's face growing more and more scarlet with each question. I was impressed with CindeeRae's investigative instincts, which, coupled with her inherent drive to protect everyone on our team, made for an especially tortured interview. I almost felt sorry for Madeleine. But then I remembered how Madeleine once emptied all her lunch garbage onto our table while Catelyn laughed, and I didn't feel quite so bad anymore.

We stopped at the intersection at the edge of West

Highland to wait for March's instructions, but he just rested on his bicycle seat, his eyes glazed over in thought. Genki pulled at his leash, ready to run ahead, and then whined when we sat through one whole traffic-light cycle.

"Where are we going, March?" I asked, hoping to snap him out of it. The sun broke over the horizon, casting a golden glow between the buildings and tree branches. Even so, the sky overhead was still a deep purple, and the streets were empty except for a trickle of cars.

"I think there's a comic book store a few blocks down." He pointed away from West Highland. CindeeRae, Madeleine, and I exchanged looks.

"You want to check it out?" Madeleine leaned over her handlebars to look down the street, as if she could see the store from where we waited.

"I think we should," he said. "Let's go."

As we pedaled down the next two blocks, Sloan Lake came into view, slick as glass. Before I could admire it, March had stood on his pedals and crossed the street to where shops dotted the other side. Without warning, he took a sharp right down a side street and skidded to a stop. A flash of color caught my eye, and when I turned toward the building to see where it had come from, I let out a squeal. Genki started to bark, slobber shooting from his mouth as he pulled against his harness, toward the comic book store.

Madeleine's bike rammed into my back tire, and we both crashed to the sidewalk.

"Are you guys okay?" CindeeRae asked, hovering over us.

From the pavement, our bikes a metal heap next to me, I pointed a shaky finger at the figure standing in front of Hero Brigade.

March whispered, "Dark Writer."

Interrupted by the commotion, the vandal turned to face us. He was only a little taller than March, and his dark hoodie was pulled over his head, the bill of a red baseball cap keeping it from falling into his eyes. He wore sunglasses, and as he looked at us, he pulled a skull bandanna mask up from where it had rested on his neck. His hands were covered in black-and-white gloves speckled with a rainbow of colors. He seemed to study us with the same intensity we studied him.

Our vandal looked just like the vigilante on the cover of Dark Writer's third issue.

He had been in the middle of painting a superhero robbing a bank, a flaming red mask pulled over his eyes and a bag overflowing with bills on his back. The mural was unfinished; there was a red cape outlined on the hero's shoulders that still needed to be filled in, and rough swirls at the edge that looked like feathers. And on the chest, two capitol *P*s, the second one messy, like we had disturbed him before he had a chance to finish it.

The vandal dropped a can of spray paint and swung a hulking backpack over his shoulders. Then he grabbed a skateboard that had been at his feet and kicked off, zooming away from the store. We watched him leave, dumbstruck.

"WHAT ARE WE WAITING FOR?!" March yelled, climbing onto his bike and wobbling after our vandal.

We scrambled to follow him. I jerked awkwardly as I tried to get my bike, adrenaline coursing through my body. Genki pulled me after March until I finally gained control and stood on my pedals to speed up.

"Hurry!" March screamed, and it was loud enough that the vandal, a block ahead, turned around to see how close we were. He sped up like there were rocket boosters on his skateboard, his backpack bobbing up and down as his foot propelled him forward.

Madeleine and CindeeRae both jumped the curb to ride in the empty road so we didn't all have to share the sidewalk. March pedaled furiously after the vandal, who had already gained another half block on us.

Our Dark Writer shot from the curb of a sidewalk, flipping the skateboard beneath him and landing

131

squarely on the road as the crosswalk signal flashed red. It took us a few seconds to reach the intersection, but even then, the road was spotted with cars, and we had twenty seconds until the light would again turn green. By then the vandal was gone.

• • •

We rode our bikes back to Hero Brigade so slowly I wondered how we stayed upright.

"Guys," I said, trying to lift everyone's spirits. "We didn't catch the vandal, but we *saw* him!"

"So what," Madeleine said, leaning her bike against the post outside the comic book store. "He got away."

"He left clues." I squatted by the two spray-paint cans our vandal had abandoned, white with red-and-orange lids. The number 94 was printed on the front of the cans. "Not only do we know what he wears, but we also know what kind of paint he uses."

"Fingerprints!" CindeeRae said. "The police can collect fingerprints now."

I shook my head. "He wore gloves. Batting gloves, maybe? Our vandal knows what he's doing."

March had already called Owen on his cell phone. He was standing by the stairs leading to Hero Brigade, speaking to Owen in low tones.

Madeleine's face brightened. "We should check the skate parks. I bet he's there a lot!"

Madeleine was right; not only was our vandal an amazing artist, but he was also a killer skateboarder. He had to spend a lot of time practicing. If we knew even a little bit more about what he looked like, we might be able to search for him at local skate parks.

March joined our huddle, looking like someone had deflated his birthday-balloon bouquet. "Owen's calling the owner and then reporting it to the cops," he said. "He wants us to stay and give a statement."

We called our parents to tell them we'd be late, and sat on the curb in front of Hero Brigade to wait for the police.

Owen showed up first, still wearing flannel pajama bottoms and a Star Wars T-shirt. Miguel showed up next, nodding at Owen before going to inspect the mural.

"Too bad the owner can't salvage it somehow," Miguel said to March as he studied the graffiti, "because even I can admit it's good."

Owen scoffed, standing back like the mural had cooties. Even if Owen didn't agree, I had felt the same way the first time I saw one of the vandal's pieces. But it was obvious he hadn't had time to polish this mural. The edges were unfinished, and the details on the face were missing. I wondered why he had been out so late working on it, putting him at risk of getting caught; maybe he thought he'd be safer on a Sunday in a more isolated area of town.

"Nia's on her way," Owen told Miguel, who nodded. And then to us, he explained, "Nia's the owner." Were all these people in a special club or something?

"We'll help with the cleanup," March said.

"Definitely," CindeeRae added.

"This isn't good for business." Miguel shook his head. And then, without looking at Owen, he said, "I'm guessing it hasn't been good for you either?"

"I've started selling comics and some rare collectibles online to recoup costs." Owen released the longest, saddest sigh I'd ever heard. "I'm surviving . . . for the moment. But my store was already struggling before the hit, and all the attention is giving places like ours a bad name."

I looked at March and watched his face pale before my eyes. He shook his head and walked away from the group.

A police car finally pulled up to the store and stopped in the middle of the parking lot, like it wasn't beholden to the white lines on the concrete. A tall, skinny, pale man with straw hair and a mole on his chin looked us over. Officer Rhodes. The same cop who had accused me of planting evidence in the dognapper case. This guy *hated* me.

He walked purposefully, like a sheriff from an old western with spurs on his boots. Genki sat down in front of me, haunches up and chest puffed back, poised to protect.

When the officer saw me, he nodded his head nice and slow. "Kazuko Jones. Of course it's you."

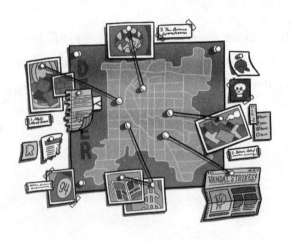

CHAPTER TWENTY-ONE

Miguel and Owen explained everything to Officer Rhodes while the policeman eyed me and March.

"Just seems a little suspicious that you two happen to be involved in this case, too." He crossed his arms over his chest. "Weren't you told not to interfere in police investigations?"

"We weren't meddling." My words came out fast and hard, a heat burning my cheeks as I said them.

Officer Rhodes pulled a notebook from his pocket. "Then what were the four of you doing riding bikes this early on a Sunday morning?"

A car pulled into the parking lot before we had time to answer.

"What the . . ." a dark-skinned woman said, stepping from the car and stalking toward the mural. She gestured at the expanse of the wall. Tattoos lined her shoulders, one of them a map of someplace magical, like the cover of a fantasy novel.

"This store was vandalized," Officer Rhodes said, turning his attention to her.

"Really?" She narrowed her eyes at the policeman, the sarcasm of her question expanding in the early morning air. "My name is Nia Tucker, and I *own* this store that was vandalized."

"These kids stumbled upon the vandal as he was defacing the storefront." Officer Rhodes gestured at the four of us huddled by our bikes. Both Owen and Miguel stepped in front of us protectively. "And I was just asking them what they were doing riding around this early on a Sunday."

Nia interrupted before we could say anything. "Excuse me, Officer? I believe the real crime happens to be painted on my wall. Someone's targeting comic book stores, and mine is the fifth to be vandalized. Could you refocus your efforts on the task at hand?"

The sun seemed to burst into the sky, glinting off a tiny green gem in Nia's nose piercing. *Whoa*, I thought. *Go, Nia.*

Officer Rhodes took a deep breath. After a few seconds, he turned his attention to the mural and began asking us about the vandal. After we told him everything we saw, March shared our biggest clue. "He uses the tag Dark Writer. It's the name of a comic book about a vigilante reporter."

I pulled my SleuthPad from my basket and powered it on, scrolling through pictures until I came to Madeleine's shot of the vandal's tag. I flashed the screen at Officer Rhodes, who glanced at it before flipping to a new page in his tiny notebook.

When he didn't say anything, March went on. "He was even dressed like Dark Writer. Black hoodie, red baseball hat, skull mask."

Owen's and Miguel's faces both lit up at that revelation. "Wow," Owen said reverently. Apparently, even if your comic book store was being vandalized by some punk, you could still respect him as long as he was inspired by an obscure comic book hero.

"What does that even mean?" Office Rhodes asked. I had to admit, it did sound confusing and not very evidence-y.

"We're not sure," March said. "But he hates comic book stores." He nodded at the mural on Hero Brigade's storefront. "And it has something to do with Dark Writer."

"I don't see that tag anywhere." Officer Rhodes cocked his head to the side.

CindeeRae puffed out a sigh of frustration. "It's not

here because we interrupted him." She patted her hand against the wall and waved it in at Officer Rhodes. When she realized her palm was still dry, she stared at it in surprise.

"It's the Montana spray paint." March gestured at the cans the vandal had left behind. "I recognize it from my research; graffiti artists use it because it dries super fast."

But I was still looking at the spot where CindeeRae's hand had been, her fingers splayed over one of the hundred-dollar bills. "Hey," I said, pointing. "Whose face is that?"

"George Washington!" CindeeRae yelped.

"He's on the dollar bill," March said.

"Alexander Hamilton?" she asked.

"That's the ten-dollar bill!"

"Benjamin Franklin . . ."

"GUYS!" I interrupted. "This isn't a history lesson. I mean, *look* at the picture and tell me who it is."

Everyone rushed to the wall, including the adults, and studied the face on the bill. March peered over my shoulder. "It's Blood Eagle."

"He's been in two murals in a row now," I said. "This superhero is stealing money with Blood Eagle's face on it. But, why?"

"Blood Eagle from the movie?" Officer Rhodes asked.

The four of us nodded.

"Well," Madeleine interrupted. "From the movie based on a comic book."

Officer Rhodes scratched something in his notebook, then took pictures of the mural and collected the spray-paint cans in a plastic bag. As he got into his car to leave, he said, "You kids aren't off the hook. Keep your noses clean, or you'll all be in big trouble."

Nia shook her head at him as he drove away. "That was the opposite of helpful."

"What does that even mean, 'keep your noses clean'?" CindeeRae asked. "Is he implying we're snot-nosed kids? Like babies?"

"No," Miguel said. "It's just a saying. It means 'mind your own business.'"

As if she had read my mind, Madeleine snapped, "If we had minded our business, he wouldn't have walked away with all those clues just now."

"Whatever," March said, his voice shaky. "They're not going to do anything with those clues anyway."

I wondered if anything the police did would be enough for March, whose face had turned tomato red. But then I realized that if they were working on my mom's case, I'd probably feel the same way. I nodded at March, and he tilted his head back at me. This was why we had to attend ComiCanon and see what clues the Dark Writer comic might hold.

Nia unlocked her store, and the Comic Club—what

I had mentally nicknamed Owen, Miguel, and Nia—headed inside.

"We'll come back to help you clean up," CindeeRae yelled after them.

Nia shook her head. "Nah," she called back. "I think I'm going to keep it for a while."

For some reason, the thought made me smile. We grabbed our bikes and took one last look at the mural before riding away.

CHAPTER TWENTY-TWO

On Monday night, Mom, Dad, and I sat together in the basement, binge-watching the third season of *Avatar: The Last Airbender*. Baa-chan had gone grocery shopping with a neighbor, and the rest of us decided to hold the first official Jones Family Party Night we'd had in weeks, complete with buttered popcorn sprinkled with chocolate chips.

I snuggled on the Lovesac with Genki while Mom and Dad sat in the corner of the couch, Mom leaning back into his chest with her legs stretched out on the cushions. It felt almost like normal, except Mom had been wearing those same pajamas all week. Still, we had to start somewhere, and rooting against the fire-benders as a family seemed fitting somehow.

Between episodes, Dad asked, "How much money did you make at the car wash and bake sale?"

"One hundred and twenty-seven dollars and fifteen cents!"

"Whoa," Mom said, looking back at me. "That's a lot of money!"

"I'm pretty sure Madeleine's mom bribed all their rich friends to come." Genki lay in a ball at my feet, and when I reached my foot out to scratch his ear, he stretched and arched his chest in my direction. When my toes dug into his armpit in just the right spot, his back leg pedaled like he was waving at the world.

"What are you going to do with it?" Mom asked.

I sat up, excited to break it down for them. "ComiCanon tickets are fifteen dollars for kids twelve and under. So that's sixty dollars it'll take to get us in. And if we have to pay for our chaperone, that'll be a hundred and ten dollars total, leaving seventeen dollars and fifteen cents for treats." March had already contacted the comic book vendor who verified he had a complete set of Dark Writer comics he would let us read, as long as no one bought them before we showed up to his booth and we gave him something valuable he could hold on to as collateral until we finished reading them. Also, he had to witness us sanitize our hands before touching the comics.

"What's the big deal about ComiCanon?" Dad asked.

"The vandal signs his graffiti as Dark Writer, which is the name of a rare comic book that's out of print. We haven't been able to find it anywhere, and some guy at ComiCanon is selling them." I stopped rubbing at Genki's armpit, and he stood to amble closer, a string of drool hanging from his jowl and over my head. I tried to push him back, but he leaned all his weight against my hand and broke free, collapsing onto my chest. I released a huff of air and wiped the slobber from my neck. "March thinks the comic might have clues about what the vandal is planning to do next."

"I'll take you guys." Dad started the next episode like it was settled. "And you don't even have to pay for my ticket."

"Really?"

"Sounds like fun," he said. "I just need to come up with a costume."

"What?" I shuddered as I remembered his last Halloween costume, Super Saiyan Goku from *Dragon Ball Z*. "You don't have to dress up."

"But cosplay is the best part about ComiCanon." Dad's voice was a little whiny.

Mom's head tipped back as she laughed. "It's happened already, honey," she said. "Our daughter is embarrassed to be seen with us."

"Only when you dress up like a weirdo," I said.

Even though I'd never been before, I knew cosplay was the best part of ComiCanon. Some people took months building their costumes, using materials like clay, Plexiglas, PVC pipe, felt, and this strange craft foam you could mold with the high setting of a hair dryer. Two years ago, March's dad spent months preparing a gigantic cosplay of the Iron Giant with built-in stilts that made him over ten-feet tall. March had plastered a picture of him onto his English journal and kids had talked about it for months.

The thought of Dad letting his nerd flag fly was a little cringy, but I also knew the unspoken rule of geekdom was allowing everyone the freedom to cosplay as they chose. It was their credo or something.

"Aren't *you* dressing up like a weirdo?" Dad asked.

"Maybe," I answered. As soon as March suggested this operation, I knew exactly what my cosplay would be: Galaxigator, a space detective in an old comic book from the fifties. March had told me all about her when he had first gotten into comic books, and now was my chance to play an investigator for the universe. Since Dad was so enthusiastic about cosplay, maybe he'd help me find the silver bodysuit, fishbowl helmet, and monocle I would need.

"Well," Mom said, sitting up. "I'm glad you're doing something exciting."

"Where are you going?" I asked as she stood up.

"All this ComiCanon talk has worn me out," Mom said, walking past me to the stairs. "But don't let me stop the fun. You two keep partying for me."

I looked at Dad, hoping he would stop her, but he just shrugged and patted the empty seat next to him. "Let's at least finish this episode."

We watched in silence for a few minutes, Prince Zuko getting angstier as the episode progressed. Then I said, "Mom's getting better, right?"

"Of course she is, Bug," he said.

"So can't Baa-chan go home now?" It felt mean to ask, but as long as she was here, it meant Mom was still sick and things were different.

Dad chuckled. "I actually thought Baa-chan was settling in nicely. She's been really helpful, and you seem to enjoy having her around."

"I do," I said, and meant it. If Baa-chan lived closer we could see her all the time and not just when Mom wasn't feeling well. I sank back into the couch and stared at the screen.

"I'm actually feeling tired," I said as the episode ended. "I'm gonna go to bed."

As if he'd understood what I'd said, Genki jumped from the Lovesac, wagging his tail, and waited for me at the bottom of the stairs.

"But we only have two more episodes to go until the one about the blood-bender."

"Maybe next time," I said. I felt much heavier going up the stairs than I had coming down.

CHAPTER TWENTY-THREE

Aside from March and my daily practice-site search, the team didn't work on the case much that week. Besides, CindeeRae was getting busier with rehearsals, and March refused to cancel his Sorcery plans. We all decided to use the downtime to prepare for ComiCanon that weekend.

On Friday, I sat on a bench in the school foyer, clutching my backpack to my chest. After our long search for the practice site that morning, March had missed the bus, so I had walked into school alone. Now I was just waiting for CindeeRae or Madeleine.

Carefully pulling my SleuthPad from the padded pocket in my backpack, I looked through all the work I had done on Mom's case. Even though Baa-chan hadn't told me what was wrong with Mom, she had given me a very important clue: Mom wasn't physically sick, but heartsick. I leaned back on the bench and looked at the ceiling, wondering what that meant.

Ten minutes before the first bell, Madeleine walked inside, followed by Catelyn and Elesha. Catelyn snickered behind her, just loud enough for Madeleine to hear, and I caught the sad tug on Madeleine's lips before she saw me. Looking relieved, she cut across the foyer and sat down next to me, muttering under her breath, "I can't stand her."

I watched Madeleine take off her backpack and adjust her hoodie.

She caught me watching her. "What?"

"You used to be friends." I nodded as Catelyn passed by. "What happened?"

Madeleine held her backpack to her chest, mirroring me, and leaned against the wall. "We just stopped hanging out," she said. "It's no big deal."

"But it *is* a big deal," I said. "I saw you with Catelyn the day your dog disappeared. You were best friends, and now Catelyn is being mean to you. There *has* to be a reason."

Madeleine looked at the ceiling, her eyes glassy. Everything she wasn't saying hummed in the air between us, like static ready to spark.

"It's okay," I said. "You don't have to tell me."

She surprised me with her quick response. "After we solved the dognapping case, I just wasn't into soccer. I thought, if I could get more excited about solving clues than I did playing a sport, maybe there were other things I might like to do, too. When I talked to my mom about it, she suggested I take a break and try new things. So I quit. And it made Catelyn so mad she quit being my friend."

I tried to imagine how I'd feel if March decided not to be my best friend anymore, and my stomach churned at the thought. We watched kids walk by, the foyer getting louder as students came from the drop-off lane and the last of the buses. I looked at the clock; the first bell would ring in five minutes.

"I'm sorry," I said, worried that she couldn't even hear me.

"It's not *your* fault." She shrugged. "I guess I changed too much, and Catelyn didn't want to be my friend if it meant we couldn't play soccer together anymore."

It was weird to think that quitting soccer would threaten a friendship. Changing just seemed to be a part of life, of growing up. I thought real friends should last, even if you decided to like different things.

"I'm glad you're trying something new," I admitted. "I like having you on *our* team."

"Thanks." Madeleine blushed. "Me too."

Madeleine had shared a big secret with me, and for

the first time I wanted to share mine. For weeks, the mystery of Mom's sickness had swollen in my chest like a dark sponge, soaking up all my fear and expanding so that it seemed there was no room for anything else. I took a deep breath.

"My mom's been sick lately, and I think she's depressed. But I don't know how to help her feel better."

"Have you asked her what's wrong?"

"No. She's so different lately," I said. "I don't even know how I'd bring it up. But I asked my dad and my grandma, and they won't tell me."

"I'm sorry." Madeleine took a deep breath and blew it out slowly, like she was in the middle of a meditation exercise. "Everybody has something."

I noticed how her eyebrows came together thoughtfully. It's like Madeleine had stopped being a bully to become one of those therapy talk-show hosts.

"What do you mean?" I asked.

March pushed through the front doors, speed-walking to the stairs. His eyes were wide and his hair extra-springy. When he saw us, he changed course and zipped toward us.

"Everybody has something to worry about." Madeleine finished her thought just as March reached us, and I almost forgot what we had been talking about in the first place.

"Guess what?" he asked.

Madeleine and I both sat up taller. "What?" we said at the same time, ready for a breaking lead in the case.

"I finally decided what I want to wear to ComiCanon." His face was set, like he was sharing one of the secrets to the universe.

Madeleine and I looked at each other.

"What?" he said. "Cosplay is serious business."

The bell rang and we stood, walking toward the stairs. When he didn't come with us, Madeleine shouted, "What, March? What are you going to be?"

"Dark Writer." His head nodded up and down like a bobble-head doll. "Brilliant, right?"

CHAPTER TWENTY-FOUR

I was drinking the rest of my chocolate milk at the kitchen bar when Dad walked in dressed as the spookiest Spider-Man villain, Venom. Baa-chan had painted a creeptastic mouth that stretched across his face, from ear to ear. It hung open, the teeth long and jagged, outlined with bloody red gums.

The milk nearly shot from my nose.

"Scary, right?" When he spoke, his own mouth appeared beneath the paint.

"You did that, Baa-chan?" I asked.

She smiled proudly, although her eyes went a little buggy when she glanced at the rest of his costume, like he had pranced out in his underwear. I mean, he basically had. The tight black-and-silver bodysuit covered his whole body, with padded muscles on his stomach and chest. His hands ended in long, clawed fingers, and a huge white spider splayed across his chest.

"Doesn't Venom wear a doctor's coat or something?" I asked, hoping he might have forgotten part of his costume upstairs.

"You're thinking of the Lizard," he said. "Okay, you ready?"

"Yes." I stood in my gray moonboots, clomping into the kitchen to put my cereal bowl in the sink. When I was done, I zipped the silver bodysuit to my neck and put the plastic fishbowl helmet with a vented mouthpiece over my head. Baa-chan had already painted a monocle over one eye.

"You look fantastic!" Mom stood in the entryway wearing a T-shirt and yoga pants; it was the first time I'd seen her wearing something other than pajamas in a couple of weeks. "We have to get a picture of you two."

Dad and I leaned together, my helmet bonking into his mega-chest. Mom smiled behind her phone, her hair slick and perfectly straight. A happy bloom expanded in my heart.

"Say 'cheese,'" Mom said, and I couldn't help but grin wide, competing with Dad's sinister Venom smile.

• • •

March couldn't contain himself in the car. "We're. Going. To. ComiCanon!" He punched one fist forward with each word, bounding in the front seat as he did. Then he turned to check out everyone's costumes.

Madeleine wore a long blue T-shirt with a gold lightning bolt on the front over red leggings and a long red scarf wrapped around her neck. To top it off she had gigantic foam fists that she had been gesturing with dramatically since she had gotten into the car.

"What's with the Hulk hands?" I asked, my fishbowl helmet in my lap.

March interrupted before Madeleine could answer, pulling the skull bandanna from his mouth to say, "Ms. Marvel, alter ego Kamala Khan, was exposed to the Terrigen Mist when she was young, which transformed her into a polymorph who can stretch her body however she wants or needs."

"So, Ms. Marvel?" I clarified.

Madeleine glared at March for stealing her thunder, the mask painted around her eyes scrunching in the corners.

I laughed. "You can punch him with your polymorph fists anytime you want."

CindeeRae, who was dressed as a gender-bent Alexander Hamilton—from the Broadway musical, of course—leaned around me. "Maybe we should keep them in the tree house. You know, in case you two decide to fight again." March scoffed and Madeleine smiled while CindeeRae adjusted her fluffy collar under a long blue velvet coat with tails.

After paying for our tickets and elbowing our way into the convention center, we stopped in the middle of the swarming crowd, our mouths gaping. It was like we had teleported into a magical world where all the characters ever created lumbered around eating jumbo pretzels and hot dogs, their free hands juggling bedazzled staffs, shields, oversize weapons, or plain old backpacks. There was body paint and costumes with fur, feathers, glitter, armor, gears, and robot parts.

It was hard to move around without bumping into people, and I accidentally rammed into a Hagrid who bowed gracefully before stepping around me. We broke through a crew from Star Trek and walked past a gathering of Spider-Men. People stopped each other for pictures; another Ms. Marvel asked Madeleine for a selfie, and they both posed with their arms up, like they were ready to box. Then we followed Dad up and down the vendor aisles as he studied a map listing all the booths and their sellers. The cardboard at the bottom of his fake Venom boots flapped against the cement as he walked.

"Where will we find this comic you're looking for?"

he asked for the second time, the roar of the crowded convention center making it difficult to hear him.

"MatchBook Comics." March speed-walked to keep up with Dad so he could study the map with him. He pointed at a purple square. "Right there." The map was color-coded, with purple standing for comic books.

Dad stopped to get his bearings, turned the map a couple of times, and walked back the way we had come, March still at his side. CindeeRae, Madeleine, and I shuffled behind them.

We passed booths with jewelry, socks, buttons and pins, comic prints, paintings, books, hats, and even shoe-laces. My fishbowl helmet started to steam up, and I took it off and carried it under one arm like an astronaut. Cosplayers held up merch from their favorite fandoms, oohing and aahing like they'd stumbled upon treasure, or at the very least evidence that there were people out there just as nerdy as them.

Now I knew why March loved it here. At school he was the lone nerd, the walking comic book know-it-all who was usually mocked whenever he talked about the things that excited him. Here, he was one among many, surrounded by warrior geeks who proudly paraded their unusual obsessions. I had understood why March was so upset by the idea of the Super Pickle closing, but for the first time I really felt how devastating it must be for him.

ComiCanon was only once a year. But the Super Pickle was there whenever he needed it. There may not be crowds of cosplayers, but Owen and his customers liked what March liked and would never make fun of him for it. Stopping the vandal meant he could keep the Super Pickle as his safe place.

We turned into a large display at the corner booth: MatchBook Comics. People swarmed around us as we cased the place. A banner with the store's name was strung high above the backdrop, which was plastered with glossy prints of comic book covers. The floor was crowded with long tables, heaped with boxes of comic books with tabbed dividers organizing them.

March pushed his way through the crowded aisle to a bearded guy manning the booth from behind a card table. The man stood, watching customers meander around the tables, wearing a Superman shirt that hugged his belly. A calculator app was displayed on his phone.

"I'm March Winters," March squeaked. "And I emailed you about looking at your Dark Writer series."

At first the man looked a little distracted by Dad, eyeing his Venom mouth. March raised his voice and repeated his request.

The man finally turned to March, a crease between his brows. "You're a kid." It was more a statement than a question.

"Yes?" March responded.

You could almost see the man revisiting his email exchange with March in his head, analyzing it to see how he had mistaken him for an adult. "What, exactly," he said slowly, "did you bring for collateral?"

When March didn't answer right away, the man looked at Dad as if waiting for him to dig a bag of blue diamonds from his bodysuit or something. Dad shrugged, and March opened his backpack. He pulled out a large carrying case shaped like Star Wars' C-3PO. Sparkling and shiny, the golden case didn't have one ding or scratch. Opening it like a briefcase filled with thousand-dollar bills, March showed the man all the action figures packed neatly inside. The man raised his eyebrows and bowed his head in appreciation of March's treasure, then pointed us toward the back table, where a teenager stood.

"Dark Writer will be in those boxes. Josh will let you read the comics behind the tables, and when you're done, you can come back and grab your collateral."

We walked to the table single file, Madeleine following March with her mega-fists and clearing us a wide path. Four boxes covered the table, and a small group stood around waiting their turn. Josh took requests from people in line before riffling through the boxes and handing them comics, along with an invoice. When it was our turn, Josh exchanged a pointed look with Bearded Guy and then led us behind the tables to a spot on the floor. Before handing us the stack of comics, he squirted a dot of hand sanitizer into each of our palms and waited for us to clean them.

Dad hung back and told us to stay put while he grabbed a snack. March gave us each a comic, and we began to read.

CHAPTER TWENTY-FIVE

The story wasn't all that different from what we had expected after seeing the comic book summaries Mrs. Davis had given us. Sam Wellerby was an unsuspecting reporter covering the appearance of several superheroes in his crime-ridden city of Silversage. In the first issue, the dark superhero, who looked almost exactly like vintage Blood Eagle, began a sloppy introduction to hero work—stopping burglaries, abductions, and assaults on unsuspecting citizens. But when he stepped in to prevent a mob hit on a local business, tearing pillars from the building to launch at the assailants, he accidentally collapsed the whole place and killed Sam Wellerby's sister, an innocent bystander. And everyone else. This incident moved Sam to assume the alias Dark Writer and work to end all superhero activity in Silversage.

By the third issue, Sam had fully assumed the Dark Writer persona and began to track down the Blood Eagle look-alike. In each of the final two issues, the series showcased a new superhero for Dark Writer to battle. The Blood Eagle look-alike never appeared again, and as far as we could tell, nothing in the comic could help us predict where our vandal might strike next. Regardless, Madeleine took pictures of each issue's cover, front page, and dark vigilante drawings for our records.

While I took notes in my SleuthPad, Madeleine approached Josh and asked if we could look at the first edition of Blood Eagle. He only had one volume, but he let us read it after we returned the Dark Writer set.

Madeleine held a picture of the vigilante on her phone next to the image from a first edition Blood Eagle comic.

"They're exactly alike," March said. "The purple costume, the metal helmet, the bony wings. That's Blood Eagle!"

"But what does it mean?" CindeeRae asked, her puffy collar ruffling as she spoke.

"Artists work on different comics all the time," March said. "Maybe an artist reused an old character from Dark Writer, since it didn't go anywhere?" He flipped to the front page and moved his finger down the list of people responsible for creating the comic.

"What are you looking for?" CindeeRae asked.

"The Blood Eagle artist," March answered. "Maybe the artist for Blood Eagle is the same one who worked on Dark Writer."

Madeleine searched through her pictures of the Dark Writer comic, selecting the one she had taken of the front page. When she found it, she flashed it back at him.

"Huh," he said, comparing the pages.

"Huh, what?" CindeeRae asked.

"The artists are different," March said. "Claudia Reed is Dark Writer's artist and Marty Cavalier is Blood Eagle's artist."

I leaned back, deflated. Every clue we found led to another dead end.

"Anyone up for nachos?" Dad called from the edge of the booth, precariously balancing three orders on two outstretched arms. Bearded Guy narrowed his eyes at Dad.

CindeeRae stood and said, "I'm starving."

I followed, stomping out the tingling in my toes.

"What do we do now?" March didn't move, obviously frustrated this operation hadn't cracked open the case.

Madeleine madly took pictures of the Blood Eagle comic, including the front page March had just examined. "There may be tons of clues here; we just haven't had time to look them over yet."

"Yeah," I agreed. "We can't give up that easily."

"Who said I'm giving up?" March huffed and went to grab his action figure case from Bearded Guy, not waiting for us to catch up.

• • •

We sat in the food court, eating our nachos and trying to guess the characters surrounding us. An entire Avengers set sat at the table to our right, and I tried not to laugh at ginormous Thor dipping single fries into a small cup of ketchup, his hammer resting on the table next to him. Dad was excited to see a family of *Avatar* characters trying to decide what to eat, and even stopped them as they passed to take a picture. A group of Deadpools did yoga just off the concession stand, and even March pulled himself from his funk to chase after the Catbus from *My Neighbor Totoro*.

We all followed him, leaving our empty nacho baskets behind to walk up and down the vendor aisles.

"I have ten dollars," CindeeRae said. "And I saw a print of the *Hamilton* cast as comic book characters on our way in." We trailed behind her; even Dad seemed to be slowing down.

"There's just something about the Blood Eagle comic." Madeleine walked between me and March. "It reminds me of the last vandal hit."

"What?" I asked. "The money?"

"No," she said. "The letters on the superhero's chest."

CindeeRae had fallen back to rejoin the conversation. "PP?" March asked.

"I don't think that second letter was supposed to be a *P*," I said. "It looked like we interrupted the vandal at the exact moment he was finishing that letter. There was a small tail on the *P*, like it was supposed to be a *B* or an *R*."

"Or an eight," CindeeRae interrupted, excited.

Madeleine stopped walking. "Say that again," she said.

"*P8*," CindeeRae said. "It could be an eight, which would make it *P8*."

"No, not *that*," Madeleine said. "What Kazu said *before* that. Say it again."

"It looked like it was supposed to be either *PB* or *PR*," I said. "Not *PP*."

"The spine!" Madeleine squealed. "I think there was a *PR* on the spine of Blood Eagle."

"It's probably for Phoenix Rising," March said matter-of-factly. "The Blood Eagle publisher."

"We need to go back," I said, yanking Madeleine

and CindeeRae around. March had already changed direction, bulldozing back to the MatchBook Comics booth.

"What's going on?" Dad asked, trying to catch up.

"Nothing," I said. "We just have to follow a clue."

We pushed back in the opposite direction, working against the crowd. Dad seemed especially awkward with his flapping cardboard feet. When we reached MatchBook Comics' booth again, Bearded Guy waved us back to Josh, and we stood in a long line waiting our turn for one more glance at the spine of Blood Eagle's first edition.

Someone behind me hollered, "Galaxigator?!" I turned to see Nia, the owner of Hero Brigade, dressed like Snow White but holding a blue, scuffed Star Wars helmet with a big red bow on top. Her black hair hung in spiral curls, and the gem in her nostril had been changed out for a miniature apple.

"Snowba Fett!" Madeleine yelled. CindeeRae turned around, laughing with us at the genius of her outfit.

"That's amazing, Nia," I said.

"You kids are hard-core." She admired our costumes and then asked if she could get a picture with me, explaining that she had inherited the entire Galaxigator series from her grandfather and refused to sell it. "She's my favorite space detective!" she said. I wondered how many more space detectives there were as I put my fish-bowl helmet back on.

I struck my space detective pose: peering into the distance and shading my eyes with my hand, which hit the plastic of my helmet with a heavy *thunk*. CindeeRae laughed as Madeleine snapped our picture.

Nia thanked me and said, "Tell Owen that you want to play your next round of Defender at Hero Brigade." I remembered that since the vandal case, Owen had been too busy trying to save his store to host March's favorite role-playing game. "I make a great Game Master."

We said good-bye and turned back to March, who was standing at the front of the line, his Dark Writer hoodie pulled over his head and his skull bandanna covering his face. Josh searched through boxes, pulling out a comic he then handed to March, who turned to leave and slammed into CindeeRae.

"Hey!" she said. "Be careful."

That's when I realized *this* Dark Writer was taller than March. He held a stack of comics to his chest, and on the very top sat the vintage volume of Blood Eagle we were looking for, *PR* printed on the spine in bulky black lettering.

Our vandal.

This Dark Writer leaned over me and glared, and I knew he recognized us from when we caught him vandalizing Hero Brigade. He moved so suddenly that I ducked, afraid he was going to hit me, but instead he pushed around us and through the crowd, surging from the booth and past Bearded Guy, who was collecting money at the card table. When the vandal glanced back, he looked directly at me before shooting into the crowd.

CHAPTER TWENTY-SIX

"**H**ey, wait!" Bearded Guy yelled as Dark Writer ran from the convention center, his green backpack bobbing behind him.

The *real* March rushed to where we stood, his bandanna down around his neck. "What just happened?" His hoodie was still pulled over his red hat, and sweat glistened on his forehead.

Madeleine pointed with her super-fists. "Our vandal just stole the comic books and left."

March stood dazed for a couple seconds, searching the crowd for our vandal. "STOP!!" he finally screeched as he caught sight of him running through the crowd. March jolted after him, the action figures in his backpack rattling as he went.

I pulled off my fishbowl helmet, handed it to Dad, and chased after March. CindeeRae and Madeleine followed. We darted through the crowd, circling around a Pokémon gathering, and paused to search for March.

"There he is!" I pointed to the black hoodie on the escalator. We elbowed our way through the horde until we were right behind him.

Our vandal was nowhere in sight, but we followed March down the hall anyway until we reached the stairwell on the opposite end of the convention center.

"He's gone." March kicked the wall. "It's no use." He yanked the hood from his head and threw the red baseball hat down the stairs, mumbling to himself as he paced back and forth.

I had never seen March so mad before. Maybe he'd calm down if we kept talking. "It looked like he took all the issues of Dark Writer and the first edition Blood Eagle," I said.

"I thought he hated comics." Madeleine said. And she had a point. Why would a vandal who hated comic book stores steal a stack of comics?

Dad huffed toward us. When he reached the stairwell, he bent over to catch his breath, one hand clutching his side while the other held my fishbowl helmet. "What the heck was that about?" The face paint on his cheek was smeared and his hair tousled, making him look even creepier.

"We think our vandal just stole all the comics we read this morning," I answered.

"Why?" he asked.

"Who knows?!" March shrieked.

"We need to make sure that's what he took." If March was too upset to take charge right now, I would have to do it. "Let's go talk to Bearded Guy at MatchBook Comics."

Dad looked exhausted at the suggestion. "Let's take a little breather first."

The four of us rolled our eyes and walked Venom to a bench where he could rest.

• • •

"I think our vandal's mad at Phoenix Rising," Madeleine blurted as we drove home, March in the front seat while us girls sat in back.

Madeleine had been scrolling through her pictures, stopping on the unfinished Hero Brigade mural. There was a reason she had made the connection between the letters on the Blood Eagle spine and the letters on the superhero's chest—the font and color were almost the same. Also, the feather shape of brushstrokes on the hero's back and the red and orange colors of his costume were identical to the phoenix in the publisher's logo.

"Then why has he been vandalizing comic book stores?" CindeeRae asked from the center seat.

"I don't know," Madeleine said. "But the hit at Hero Brigade is the first time he identified someone specific. There's got to be a reason."

"Maybe he's mad at both," CindeeRae said. "I can be mad at lots of people at the same time."

Madeleine and I turned to look at her.

"What?" she said. "I can."

Dad turned up the radio as he took the off-ramp from the freeway onto Federal Boulevard.

"I told you," March said, raising his voice. "We can't get distracted by why he's mad or what it all *means*. We're trying to *find* the vandal, not *psychoanalyze* him."

I snapped, "If we figure out *why* our vandal's mad, we'll be that much closer to catching him."

"Guys!" CindeeRae held her arms out. "No fighting."

March ignored her, shaking his head and grumbling, "I told you, that won't help. We need to focus on clues about his identity."

After all the detecting work we had done together, I couldn't believe we disagreed about something this important.

CindeeRae caught my hardened expression and held up a threatening finger. "I mean it," she said. "If it causes a fight, we don't talk about it anymore."

"Whatever." I sat back in my seat and looked out my window.

We rode on in silence, Dad drumming his fingers on

172

the steering wheel to the song on the radio. I watched the buildings alongside the road pass in a blur and felt the same anxiety I had over Mom's case swell in my chest, only this time over my fight with March. I worried that there might actually be something big enough to ruin our friendship forever. When we dropped CindeeRae off, March was snoring from the front seat, and I wondered if he even really cared at all.

Madeleine leaned toward me and whispered, "Does your mom feel better?"

At first I was confused why she would ask me that, and then I remembered telling her about Mom.

"Not really," I answered, checking Dad's expression to see if he could hear us. "I just wish I knew what was making her sad."

Madeleine leaned back in the seat and closed her eyes. "And you already asked your dad?"

The knot in my chest tightened, and I swallowed down the lump in my throat, glad she wasn't looking at me. "Yes, but he wouldn't say."

I watched as Dad sang along to a bouncy song on the radio, his human teeth glowing against the face paint.

"Have you tried asking your mom yet?" Madeleine opened her eyes and looked at me. "I mean, she would know what's wrong better than anyone, right?"

Madeleine had asked me that already, but the Mom with bedroom sickness seemed different from the Mom I had known before, and it scared me a little to think about confronting her. Besides, wasn't it my job as a detective to find out what her sickness was? To track down all the clues and then solve the puzzle myself?

I shrugged. "Then why hasn't she told me?"

Madeleine closed her eyes again, and when she spoke, her words sounded sleepy. "Maybe she hasn't told you because you haven't asked."

CHAPTER TWENTY-SEVEN

On Monday, March and I started investigating the area around the Super Pickle. Two weeks into our search and we hadn't found the practice site. I had been detecting for a couple years and knew sleuthing out clues sometimes took a while, but this particular operation was starting to feel like the biggest waste of time.

March blacked out the area we had searched on the map, and we started the ride back home.

"Owen's making hardly any money online. We need to figure out a way for him to stay open." He huffed, the effort to talk while pedaling made him winded.

"But, um, that's not our job," I said. When I realized how cold that sounded, I quickly added, "Solving the case is the best way to help Owen, right?"

"There's more than one way to help him," he snapped, and then started complaining about the vandal.

"Everyone has something," I called over my shoulder, remembering what Madeleine had told me before.

"What's that supposed to mean?" he grumbled, catching up with me so that we rode side by side.

"Everyone has something to worry about." I weaved to the edge of the sidewalk. "Even comic book villains. And our vandal. Maybe he does what he does because he has a good reason to be upset."

"Who cares?" Even though he wasn't yelling, his voice was loud in the early morning. "He's doing lots of damage."

I thought about all the comic book stories March had ever shared with me. "What about *Colonel Nightmare and the Sandstorm of Retaliation*?" It was one of March's favorite comics, about a mutant scientist who punished the government with a sand tornado because an undercover operation to robotize the military had killed his family.

"What about it?"

"Colonel Nightmare was angry that his family had been killed and was trying to stop the government from killing more people."

"So what?"

"He sounds like a bad guy, but he's just trying to make things right." I thought about all the vandal's work, and the way the bad guys in his pictures were dressed like superheroes. Maybe he was trying to right some wrong, a wrong that had hurt him somehow.

"Colonel Nightmare is a vigilante," March said, as if that explained everything. We turned off Federal Boulevard, riding along Lakeview Park toward my house.

I didn't respond, and March sighed, as if he was bracing himself for a face-off. "And vigilantes take the law into their own hands because they believe something isn't fair. Like with Colonel Nightmare—he didn't think the government was ever going to pay for their mistake, so he punished them himself."

"Like Dark Writer, who was working against the superheroes to try and stop other people from getting killed like his sister." When March shook his head, I said, "What if our vandal is a vigilante like Dark Writer, serving justice to someone who hasn't had to pay for a big mistake?"

"But what has Owen done wrong?" he asked. "Or Miguel? Or Nia?"

"I don't know." I slowed down as we neared my house.

"Whatever," March said, not even stopping to say good-bye. I watched him disappear as he rounded the block.

• • •

The next day, Madeleine and I sat at a long table, studying all the Street Artist case files on my SleuthPad. We had both snuck into the library during lunch to see if we could figure out why our vandal held a grudge against Phoenix Rising. March had made it clear he didn't want to talk about it, and we couldn't tip CindeeRae off about going behind his back. So Madeleine and I had decided to investigate this lead on our own, telling them we were working on a group project for social studies instead.

We were the only kids in the library, and Mrs. Davis sat behind the nearby checkout counter crunching on baby carrots. Madeleine and I quietly ate our own lunches as we worked, examining her pictures on my SleuthPad of the Dark Writer's front page. It didn't take long for us to realize only two people had done all the work for the comic. Claudia Reed was the artist, but she had also co written the story with Marty Cavalier.

"They sound familiar," Madeleine whispered as Mrs. Davis grabbed a book and headed our way. We both leaned into each other as Madeleine scrolled through images on her phone and stopped on one, zooming in on an image of Blood Eagle's front page and pointing the screen at me. I pulled it close to read the tiny print as Mrs. Davis shelved the book behind our table.

"Marty Cavalier was the Blood Eagle artist," I murmured to myself. "That's why the hero from Dark Writer looks exactly like first-edition Blood Eagle. He had totally seen it and used it for another comic."

Mrs. Davis grabbed a school iPad from the bin and ducked to our table. "I'm sorry, girls. I hate to interrupt," she said. Even so, she pulled out a chair and got comfortable. "But I couldn't help but overhear and thought I'd remind you of some research I presented at our last meeting." Mrs. Davis was my kind of nosy.

She pushed the school iPad toward us, the article from the *Denver Accolade* displayed on the screen.

"That's about the Denver company that published Dark Writer," I said. We had talked about it at our last team meeting.

"Yes, Relic Comics," Mrs. Davis said, her dark eyes serious. "But have you read the whole article?"

Madeleine and I skimmed the screen together, both of us stopping on the second paragraph. "Claudia Reed and Marty Cavalier were co-owners of Relic Comics. They didn't just work together on this comic book; they worked together on an entire comic book business."

We stared at a thumbnail of Marty and Claudia at the very bottom of the page, the two of them smiling. Marty's dark hair was slicked back, like a superhero, and he stood like he was holding his breath, his chest puffed out. He looked a lot like the goofy guy in the Super Pickle mural, taking money from the miniature

Blood Eagle. In the picture, Claudia sat next to Marty on a stool, her head barely reaching his shoulder and her curly hair wild around her head.

"After hearing what you two had discovered"—Mrs. Davis nodded at the iPad—"I thought you might find that interesting."

"It is!" Madeleine said. "Thank you."

"Yeah. Thanks, Mrs. Davis." I typed some notes into my SleuthPad as Madeleine gathered her things.

Once the librarian was out of earshot, I leaned close to Madeleine and whispered, "Marty Cavalier took credit for Blood Eagle. And now that it's super famous, Claudia must be steaming mad!"

Madeleine grinned. "I think we just found our motive *and* our vandal."

I stood, clutching my SleuthPad to my chest. "We'll have to figure out how to tell the rest of the team." The last thing I wanted to do was break the news that we had cracked the case without March and CindeeRae's help.

As we walked from the library, Madeleine pointed at a poster hanging in the hallway. "I was thinking about joining," she said. The art club met every Wednesday after school, and the poster promised that the art teacher would help students work on one big project of their choice. "I thought I could do photography."

"That sounds cool." I smiled at her.

"Do you want to come with me?" Madeleine's voice was soft and hesitant.

I thought about how calming it had been to do shodō with Baa-chan. The swoop of the brush as I tried to paint Japanese characters was different from watercolor but just as soothing. I understood why Baa-chan enjoyed it so much. "Sure," I said. "I can try it."

She beamed at me, tucking the phone into her back pocket as we walked up the stairs to class. Even with the thought of art club tomorrow after school, my mind couldn't help but flit back to Marty Cavalier, his name sliding under my skin like a splinter.

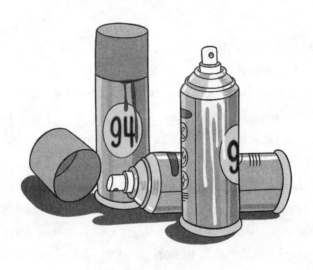

CHAPTER TWENTY-EIGHT

March waved the newspaper at me like a flag as I made my way down the bus aisle. *Uh-oh.* He had already seen it.

I slowed as I neared our seat, unsure if I was prepared for his reaction.

Before I sat down, he barked, "What does this even mean?"

That morning, after our practice-site search, I had discovered the picture buried in the local section of the newspaper. As I untucked my copy from under my arm and opened it again, I found myself hoping it had disappeared. It still didn't make any sense.

We both stared at it for a few seconds. Yep. No doubt about it. The vandal had painted our team.

In an alley downtown, March, CindeeRae, Madeleine, and I were painted standing shoulder to shoulder in our ComiCanon cosplay, staring straight ahead. Actually, scratch that. We weren't staring, because that would require eyes. Each of us had Xs where our eyeballs should have been.

"What is it?" March asked. "A warning? Is this guy going to kill us?"

"No," I said. "Street artists are about silent protest." Even as I said it, my stomach clenched painfully.

March's legs bounced on his heels as he sat, and I wished that he would calm down. Just watching him made me nervous.

"Look," I said. "He must have recognized us. He knows we're searching for him."

"You think?!" His voice was way too loud, even on a noisy school bus.

"He's just trying to scare us so we'll stop." I folded the newspaper and shoved it into my backpack.

"Well, it worked." March huffed and rolled his copy, too, sliding it into his hoodie pocket. "I think we need to suspend all operations that put us at risk of the vandal's wrath."

"What does that even mean?" I asked. "How do we solve this case by *suspending operations*?"

"Not all operations." He shrugged. "Just the ones where we're outside. In full view of, you know, the vandal."

I didn't know what to say, because it sounded to me like March wanted to quit. But we couldn't quit now that Madeleine and I had finally cracked the case. We just needed to track down Claudia Reed.

"We should talk to the team first," I said.

"Fine," he snapped, sitting back in the seat so forcefully, it released a puff of air. "We'll take a vote."

We rode the rest of the way to school in silence, March turned toward the window.

CindeeRae was waiting for us at the bus drop, waving her own copy of the paper in the air.

"I told you," March muttered as we stepped from the bus. "We need to activate safety mode."

I rolled my eyes, not even wanting to know what that meant. Before CindeeRae could say anything, I cut her off. "We'll call a vote. Okay?" I knew I sounded snappish, but detectives shouldn't be so wishy-washy. And unless Madeleine sided with me, I would be outvoted, and this case would be over. I'd be left with Mom's case, and I wasn't getting anywhere with that one.

We walked toward the school as kids swarmed around us, squealing and laughing as everyone made their way into the school.

Before we had passed the threshold to the entryway, Madeleine rushed at us, skidding to a stop with squeaky sneakers. "Did you see?" Her eye twinkled and her face split into a smile. "We've been immortalized in spray paint!"

March crossed his arms, and CindeeRae's mouth dropped open in surprise.

She went on. "It means we've been recognized as a formidable opponent," she went on. This girl was an adrenaline junkie.

I grinned. At least I knew how Madeleine would be voting.

• • •

We had gone to the library after lunch to take our official vote, and March and Madeleine looked like the two ends of the Emotion Diagram that hung in Mrs. Thomas's room: March was Mad, and Madeleine was Glad.

"Obviously," I said, my voice thick with a confidence I wasn't sure I felt, "our vandal is not going to murder us."

"That's why he's called a *vandal*," Madeleine agreed. "And not a *murderer*."

"Maybe," March said. "Maybe not. But we don't have enough clues for another operation anyway. Plus, after *that* mural, we need to avoid fieldwork for a while."

"Agreed," CindeeRae said, without waiting for a pause in the conversation. "He's already breaking the law. And once you get stuck in the dark web of crime, murder is one slippery slope away."

I almost shared the information Madeleine and I had uncovered in the library, even though we had gotten it behind their backs. Knowing that Marty Cavalier had gotten the idea for Blood Eagle when he worked with Claudia Reed was a huge clue! But if we told them about the lead we had discovered at a secret team meeting, they would know we had lied about our social studies project to avoid working with them. And that wouldn't go over very well.

Luckily Madeleine jumped in. She smirked at CindeeRae. "Who are you anyway? A double agent trying to bring down the Mafia? The only weapon our vandal uses is spray paint. This case will not be a slippery slope to murder."

Mrs. Davis shushed us from behind the checkout counter. I willed her not to come over and tell March and CindeeRae what we had discovered together.

"Look," Madeleine whispered, turning to me for backup. "We can't give up now. Let's just keep searching for the practice site and wait for more clues about *who* our vandal is," she said, appealing to March's obsession with clues about the vandal's identity.

"Yes!" I nodded at her. "We'll activate safety mode and just continue our current operation, putting a hold on future operations until we have more information."

"That sounds good." March studied the table like it was the most interesting thing he'd ever seen. "But I'd like to withdraw from the practice-site search."

"Really?" I asked. March was the one who had not only pitched this case in the first place but had proposed this operation as the best way to track down the vandal—to save Owen's store, to save *all* the comic book stores.

"No problem, partner," Madeleine said to me. "I'll search for the practice site with you."

For a second I felt off-balance, like when you're going down the stairs and expect one more step than there really are. How could March abandon *this* mission, *his* mission?

"Okay." I shrugged like I didn't care, my fingers prickling uncomfortably. "Madeleine and I will search for the practice site while you two . . ." I searched for the words and couldn't find a nicer way to say it. "Wait for something else to happen."

CHAPTER TWENTY-NINE

Art club was a small group of mostly sixth graders. I recognized Penny Miller from Madeleine's soccer team and her friend Zannie Carson, who was my reading buddy when I was in first grade. Rascal Pope from Mrs. Thomas's class was the only fifth grader I could see, and he was busy Mod-Podging newspaper print onto a giant wooden panel on a corner of the floor in the art room.

Everyone else sat at long craft tables while the school's art teacher, Mr. Maximillian, painted something bright and swirly on a canvas at the front of the room. The circles reminded me of the picture our vandal had painted of the team—our eyes white unseeing swirls covered by jagged black Xs. I shivered and shook the image from my mind.

Instrumental music played from the room's speakers but not loud enough to cover the chatter of kids as they worked.

"Ladies!" Mr. Maximillian said, without looking up. His long, wavy hair framed a perfect bald spot on the top of his head, which reminded me of a giant egg sitting in a straw nest. "Welcome to art club!"

Madeleine and I mumbled weak hellos and nodded at a couple of younger kids in front who looked up from their watercolors to smile at us. Mr. Maximillian used the corner of his apron to clean his brush, which he then dropped into the wide front pocket before walking toward us. "We're so glad you're here." He stood with his hands on his hips, surveying the bustling room proudly. "Art club is basically free time to create whatever you want. As you can see, everyone works on a project of their choosing, big or small. I'm happy to help, or not help, as much as you need."

Mr. Maximillian led us to the cabinets lining one side of the room and opened a couple so we could see inside. Paint bottles and cups full of paintbrushes crowded the shelves. "If we have the supplies, you can use them. You can also bring in your own materials, if you'd like."

He leaned over an empty table and patted the surface. "Sit wherever you want. We only ask that you follow two rules: one, clean up after yourself, and two, be kind."

"Thanks," Madeleine said, her hands twisting in front of her. "But what if I wanted to work on photography?"

"A wonderful art form!" Mr. Maximillian's face beamed. "You can use the computer in the back of the room to manipulate photos, which I can teach you how to do, or you can print off pictures you'd like to use in hard copy."

We picked our seats and set our backpacks beneath the table while Mr. Maximillian returned to his canvas at the front of the class.

"Do you mind if I work on the computer for a while?" Madeleine asked, and I shook my head, suddenly feeling like I didn't belong.

I watched her take her seat and then went back to the cabinets to search the cupboards for inspiration. On one of the shelves I found stacks and stacks of old magazines. Baa-chan had said she liked making collages with different elements she would piece together into one work of art. I grabbed a handful, found a pair of scissors, and took them back to our table.

An hour had gone by before I even realized it, my pile of magazine cutouts curling in on themselves and floating across the table. When Mr. Maximillian called time, I gathered them together and searched for an extra folder in my backpack to store them in.

"What are you working on?" I jumped at the voice.

Zannie had come up behind me quietly, carrying an easel with one hand and a canvas with the other.

"I'm not sure yet," I said. "Some kind of collage."

"Cool." She tucked her dark hair behind one ear, where I could see she had shaved the sides. Deep blue highlights were woven throughout. I wished Mom would let me experiment with my hair like that.

Penny slowed as she passed, waiting for Zannie to catch up, and Zannie followed her to the back wall where they stored their projects. When both girls turned back toward the tables, Penny said hi to Madeleine, and Madeleine's eyes lit up. I realized that maybe Catelyn was the only member of the soccer team still upset about Madeleine quitting.

Kids rinsed out brushes and put bottles of glue away while Mr. Maximillian turned off the music and walked around the room, squatting now and then to pick up stray scraps of paper.

Madeleine returned to our table with a stack of colored printouts—pictures from the vandal hits. Only she had cropped the images in interesting ways and brightened colors so they popped more. Goose bumps tingled my scalp—the same feeling I'd had looking at the vandal's murals in person.

"That's cool," I said. "What are you going to do with them?"

"I'm not sure yet." She smiled so big, dimples appeared in the center of her cheeks, and I couldn't help but grin back at her infectious happiness. "It's just exciting to try something new."

"Yeah," I said. "I kinda lost track of time."

"What did *you* work on?"

I opened the folder and showed her my magazine cutouts. "I'm going to work on a collage at first, and then maybe paint some things over it. I'm still deciding."

"That sounds very modern." Madeleine pulled her backpack from under our table.

"My grandma is an artist. She used to combine collages with stamps and original artwork," I explained, tucking the folder into my backpack and hoisting it onto my shoulders.

"So artistic talent runs in your family?"

"Maybe," I said, feeling my cheeks flush. "It would be cool if it did."

"Wish I knew if it ran in mine," Madeleine said. "Being adopted is weird sometimes. I have no idea what my biological parents are good at."

"You're obviously a natural," I said as we walked from the art room, nodding at the stack of printouts she held in her hands.

"Thanks," she said, dimples returning to her cheeks. "Art club is pretty cool."

CHAPTER THIRTY

Madeleine was sweating by the time she got to my house on her bike the next morning. I tossed her a newspaper. "Want to check if our vandal did anything last night?"

Her hair was pulled back into a tight ponytail, her jacket covering what looked like a pajama top. I smiled, remembering how she had saved me from my own pj embarrassment. While she looked through the paper, I studied March's map to see where we should search next. I picked the area closest to us and asked Madeleine, "Anything?"

"Nope." She rerolled the paper and tossed it into my basket. "Let's go."

We rode side by side down Honeysuckle, the chilly

wind blowing my hair. The peek a boo sunrise had just turned to a full sunburst when Madeleine called over to me, "How's your mom?"

"Better." Last night she had left the house to visit friends. Mom had lots of friends, and some of them had stopped by to visit after she had first gotten sick. Baa-chan had sent them all away so abruptly—trying to secure Mom's rest and well-being—that they had stopped coming over. But Mom had not only gone to see her friends last night, she had driven somewhere to do it, all by herself. That *had* to be a good sign.

"What about Catelyn?" I asked.

"She still hates my guts," Madeleine said. "But I apologized for quitting the team, and she stopped calling me names. So that's something."

I thought about how Madeleine had changed since I had gotten to know her. She went from soccer star to photography wiz, and her friendship with Catelyn hadn't been able to survive the shift. When we had first talked about it, I couldn't understand why Catelyn wasn't more accepting of Madeleine growing and transforming. But March's passion for leading this case had seemed to vanish, and I didn't want to admit how uncomfortable I was with that change. And then my mind wandered to how much the mystery illness had changed Mom. March and Mom had always been there for me. But now that the most predictable and reliable relationships in my life had shifted so quickly, it suddenly felt like I was trying to climb a mountain in the middle of an earthquake. And I didn't want to admit that I was even more worried that it wouldn't be long before their feelings about me changed, too.

We reached the freeway barrier in silence and wove through the alleys and backsides of buildings on that end of town. Finding nothing for three blocks, I slowed to a stop and turned my bike around.

"It's been twenty minutes," I said. "Let's head back."

We turned around and followed the same path home. When I looked up to cross the street, I noticed the billboard advertising *Blood Eagle: An Origin Story* on the other side of the freeway, next to the movie theater. I screeched to a stop. "What?" Madeleine asked. She used her feet to brake, and the sound of gravel crunching beneath her sneakers made me cringe.

"Look." I pointed, scrambling to grab my SleuthPad from my basket.

While Madeleine squinted at the billboard, I snapped a picture and zoomed in on my screen. She peered at my SleuthPad.

The second half of the movie title had been crossed out with red spray paint, and there was something written above it in squished, drippy letters. Blood Eagle's face had been painted over, and the bottom corner of the billboard was covered in a big Dark Writer tag.

"Can you see what it says?" I asked.

"No," Madeleine said. "But it definitely belongs to our vandal."

I nodded, feeling the anxious flutter fill my chest. "That's another clue."

"It'd be better if we could actually read it," she said, punching away at her phone. "I'm going to download a binocular app."

"Good idea." I looked over her shoulder while she found a free one and clicked to install.

"Let's ride a little closer." Madeleine stuffed her phone into her back pocket, and we biked a few blocks to where the road climbed and the barrier dipped into a grassy valley.

She skidded to another stop and pulled her phone out. "This is as close as we'll get." Squaring the billboard in the phone's frame, she magnified the image as high as it would go.

"*Origin of Deceit*?" I asked, squinting at the letters.

"I think so," Madeleine agreed, snapping a few screen shots of the enlarged image. "But what's painted over Blood Eagle's face?"

I shrugged. It was almost impossible to make out the red paint over the shadowy image, but there was definitely more to the picture than we could see from here.

"You know what this means?" Madeleine whispered,

even though no one was around to overhear. "Another operation!"

Madeleine stood on her pedals and took off ahead of me and I followed her, the nervous energy pumping through my legs as we sped home. This might be the break in the case we had all been waiting for. Even so, I worried how March would take the news. I muttered to myself, "He's not going to like this."

• • •

I had invited the team to my house that afternoon so we could study the billboard hit and plan our next operation. While everyone got settled at our dining room table, Madeleine and I told March and CindeeRae about art club and our different projects.

"Maybe you can ask Mr. Max about using spray paint as a medium," CindeeRae joked while March shifted in his seat. "I'm just saying. Maybe he knows some tricks of the trade."

"Can we get started already?" March interrupted.

Madeleine had printed copies of the blurry picture for all of us, and we sat silently, studying the image at the dining room table.

"*Origin of Deceit*?" March said at last. "What's that supposed to mean?"

"*Deceit* means 'lies, dishonesty,'" CindeeRae said knowingly. "There's a lot of deceit on Broadway."

Baa-chan brought in snacks, and the room fell silent again. She walked around the dining room, spying over our shoulders at the pictures while pushing bowls of chips and popcorn to the middle of the table. Genki pranced behind her, tail swinging like she had promised to drop him a snack. When we didn't say anything else, Baa-chan left the dining room to rummage through the refrigerator.

Genki had gotten tired of waiting and touched his nose to the table. He was tall enough to rest his head on the edge but knew he wasn't allowed. I grabbed a handful of popcorn and dropped it beneath my chair. He pushed his way under the table, flopped to the floor, and munched on the popcorn next to my feet.

"But that's not the only clue." I pointed at Blood Eagle's obscured face. "If we could see that, maybe we'd understand the rest."

"We might be able to see it if we got closer," Madeleine said.

Baa-chan walked back into the room, this time carrying a six-pack of grape soda. She pulled a can for each of us and set the rest on the table before leaning on the doorframe to listen in.

"Thanks for the snacks," Madeleine said, hinting at Baa-chan to leave.

"Do you know billboard graffiti is called a 'heaven spot'?" Baa-chan nodded toward the pictures. "Street artists love a challenge, and heaven spots are so dangerous they could send you to heaven if you're not careful."

"Thanks, Baa-chan," I said. "We didn't know that."

"You're welcome." Baa-chan pointed toward the basement. "I'll be downstairs watching *The Price Is Right*."

As soon as we heard the television snap on, CindeeRae asked, "What do you mean by *closer*?"

Madeleine lowered her voice, even though there was no chance Baa-chan could hear us. "We visit the theater and look at the billboard in person."

"What if we still can't see it?" March folded his arms across his chest.

"There's a ladder," Madeleine said, pointing at the small, thin rungs on one side of the billboard's post.

"So what?" I laughed nervously, my stomach clenching as I spoke. "We climb the billboard to see it closeup?"

CindeeRae said, "No way," just as Madeleine said, "Maybe?"

The color drained from CindeeRae's face, her freckles standing out like ink splatter. "I'm terrified of heights."

"Me t-t-too." March stuttered as he spoke, although I didn't remember him ever being afraid of heights before.

"I could do it," Madeleine said. She shrugged like

she'd just volunteered to enter a hot-dog eating contest. "We could have our parents drop us off at the theater again, only this time, instead of watching a movie, you could watch me get us another clue."

I had to remind myself to blink, my mind stuck on the image of March, CindeeRae, and me running around the base of the billboard with a cartoon safety net, ready to catch Madeleine when she fell.

"Because you want to die?" March seemed to have been taking drama lessons from CindeeRae, his mouth hanging open and his eyes wide.

"Yeah," CindeeRae said. "We don't wanna clean up *that* mess."

"Okay," I said, keeping my voice calm. "We don't even know if that will be necessary. We might be able to see the graffiti from the base of the billboard."

"What's going on here?" Dad's voice boomed behind us. We jumped.

We swung around to see him and Mom standing in the doorway. While she wasn't dressed fancy, she had leveled up from yoga pants to jeans.

"Sheesh!" Dad chuckled. "Jumpy much? What are you guys up to?"

"Homework," CindeeRae said a little too quickly.

Mom shrugged her jacket over her shoulders.

"Where are you going?" I asked.

"I'm going to visit some friends again," she said, and I smiled.

"Good-bye, kids!" Mom waved and walked toward the front door. Dad waved back and then plodded upstairs. I could hear the car hum in the driveway, and I felt like running outside to cheer her on as she drove away.

"So Operation Study Billboard Graffiti is a go?" Madeleine asked.

I nodded, reminding myself that climbing the billboard might be completely unnecessary. March and CindeeRae exchanged looks before nodding, too.

CHAPTER THIRTY-ONE

Before bed, I scrolled through pictures Madeleine had sent to my SleuthPad, admiring a new art project she had started at home, when Genki began to whimper. I sat up in my bed and froze.

My door was open, and I could hear my parents' angry voices cut from behind their door down the hall. I didn't understand—Mom had left the house tonight. Everything should have been back to normal.

I snuck out of my room and past the bathroom until I was standing just outside their door. Genki licked my fingers as I leaned closer to listen. I could just barely hear Mom say, "I'm just not ready."

"Then be honest with me about it." Dad's voice

was loud. He dropped to a low growl, as if he realized he was yelling. "Don't lie about going and then sit in the car."

I felt dizzy. I crouched into a ball at the base of the door, in case Baa-chan heard and peeked upstairs.

"No one can tell me how to process this." Mom's voice was prickly. "I don't want to go downstairs. I don't want to go back to work. I can't even manage to parent the child I have left. And I'm not ready to talk about it with a bunch of strangers."

Her words echoed in my head, getting louder and louder until my pulse throbbed in my ears. What did she mean? She couldn't even manage to parent me, the left-over child?

I rocked back onto the floor, and Genki licked my face and nuzzled my collarbone, leaving strings of slobber across my cheek. When I didn't pet him back, he nudged my chest with his nose, whimpering again until I grabbed his ears and pushed our foreheads together. The tears stung my eyes and rolled down my face and then my neck, leaving hot trails that I rubbed against Genki's sloppy jowls.

My parents continued to argue behind the door, Dad snapping at Mom about how I was still here, growing up without her. Wasn't that enough for her to return to our family?

I stood, feeling like a shaken soda bottle, the pressure building in my chest. I wanted to stomp my feet, pound their door, scream as loud as I could.

I was more confused than ever, and it didn't feel like something I could solve with more detective work. All the hope I'd been holding in my chest for Mom to get better burst into flames, pulsing through my arms and legs like lava. I raced to my room, Genki barely slipping in behind me before I closed the door. I buried myself beneath the pile of blankets on my bed and tried to shut out the fight, Genki snuggling beside me until my hiccuping sobs rocked us both to sleep.

• • •

After school on Friday, I found Baa-chan standing over a large canvas laid flat on the dining room table. Next to her was a tray of black paint, a tray of red paint, and two brushes. I stepped closer, holding my breath as I looked at the picture. It was a collage with bits and pieces of things that looked so different but fit perfectly together, like a puzzle. There was an outline of a woman's body in one swooping black curve and square stamps with kanji. In the corner was a bird the color of shallow ocean water that seemed to be flying across the canvas. The bird's skeleton was outlined in red paint, but instead of looking scary, it seemed delicate and strong at the same time.

"That's amazing, Baa-chan." My scalp tingled. The collage was uncomfortable and beautiful at the same time.

She looked up from the table as if shocked to see me. "I'm sorry, Kazu-chan! I was hoping to finish before you came home."

"That's okay." I leaned closer to look at the texture, bumpy, but shiny and mesmerizing. "I want to see."

"I haven't done this in so long," she said. "I got carried away and lost track of time."

"Can I watch?" I took off my jacket and set my backpack on the floor.

"Of course," she said. "I just need to add some kanji over here, and I'll be done for now."

I sat in the seat closest to the canvas and rested my chin in my hands as I watched her dip the brush into the paint. Her hand swirled hypnotically, and I got a little dizzy following the brush.

"What does it mean?" I asked.

"It's for your mother." She paused to meet my eyes. "You inspired me to try my artwork again. I didn't realize how much I missed it until we started talking about your street artist."

Baa-chan finished with the black paint and laid the

brush across the paint tray. She picked up the other paintbrush, dipped it in red, and added one last character to the string of kanji. "There." Her face was bright and happy.

"What does that mean?" I pointed to the red kanji that looked like a bird sitting on the top plank on a fence post: 生.

"It means 'life and growth.'" She stepped back and admired her work, then looked at me and smiled. "Your mom is feeling much better. I think it's time to schedule my flight back to Jii-chan."

My chest went cold and prickly. "But she still spends a lot of time in her room." I didn't want to admit that I'd overheard my parents fighting last night. Just a few weeks ago, I had wanted Baa-chan to leave, but now it felt like she would be abandoning me. I imagined sitting alone in the living room with no one but Genki to keep me company after she left.

"Kazu-chan," she said tenderly, and my eyes watered. "I'll be here for a couple of more weeks, at least. I'm just planning ahead. And even when I go, we'll still write and FaceTime."

I nodded, not meeting her eyes.

"Besides," she added, "I've come to realize that if I stay too long, it will take your mom even longer to get better. She needs to be able to fill the space I leave behind."

I brushed a stray tear from my cheek with the back of my hand and then reached out and fiddled with the brush absentmindedly.

"Would you like to try a little shodō before your snack and homework?"

I looked at Ba-chan, catching a shimmer in her eyes. "Can we just sit on the couch and talk instead?"

"I would love that," she said.

CHAPTER THIRTY-TWO

On Sunday night, we met in the movie theater's lobby so our parents wouldn't get suspicious, March and I waiting with twitchy hands and roaming eyes. CindeeRae skidded in still dressed in her black tights and Ladybug cape, fresh from a costume fitting. Madeleine followed her, wearing what looked like a black bodysuit, sleek running shoes, and baseball gloves. As hard as it was to upstage CindeeRae after rehearsals, Madeleine had somehow managed to do it. She looked like she was there to burgle concessions. We rushed her outside and to the side parking lot before anyone asked questions.

"What are you doing?" CindeeRae asked, gesturing to Madeleine's getup.

"Just in case," she said, pulling the gloves so they were nice and snug. "You know . . ."

"I've got a bad feeling about this," March mumbled under his breath, and I nodded in agreement.

But even still, we followed her to the top of the embankment that led to the freeway barrier. We were much closer than Madeleine and I had been when we first discovered the hit, but it was still impossible to see what had been painted over Blood Eagle's face. Madeleine stopped and pulled out her phone, activating the binocular app. "Still can't see it."

We all crowded around her. She was right. And the red spray paint against the dark background made it even more difficult to see. I squinted harder. *Nothing.*

Madeleine marched forward without a word.

We crept closer to the base of the billboard and looked up the pole, which seemed like it was one hundred stories high. From this angle, the picture was even more skewed and impossible to see. Although I was safe on the ground, my stomach fluttered at the idea of scaling that tiny ladder.

Madeleine stretched like she was preparing for a soccer game, pushing one arm up and over her back in a twisty contortion.

"This isn't really happening, right?" March asked, looking from me to CindeeRae and then to Madeleine, who was now stretching her legs. "I mean, you might not even be able to read it from up there."

I nodded, not trusting my voice to remain steady.

"I have to at least try," Madeleine said, brushing imaginary dirt from her hands and securing her phone in a zippered pocket over her heart. "Here goes nothing."

"Wait!" I held my arm out. Madeleine rested her hands on her hips while I pulled two dog leashes from my backpack. I slung one over my shoulder and then fastened the other one around her waist, pulling the hook through the handle until it was snug like a belt. She held her arms out while I worked, and then, when I was done, I dropped the hook end of the leash into her outstretched hand.

"What's this?" she asked.

"Hook it onto the rung above you each time you go up a step," I said. "That way, if you slip, it might stop you from falling."

It was as if the group let out a collective sigh.

"That's brilliant," March said, and then seemed to change his mind. "If it works."

"Still," CindeeRae interrupted, her voice steely. "This is stupid. And crazy dangerous."

When Madeleine didn't say anything, she continued, "And I want to make it clear that even though I try to be a team player, like really hard—" She stopped to look at each of us pointedly. "I don't support this operation!"

Even March raised his eyebrows at that. I waited for Madeleine to snap back, but she just nodded.

The air seemed to chill around us, and all I could hear was the swooshing of cars speeding by on the other side of the freeway barrier. Madeleine approached the ladder. Letting out a big breath, she started the long climb up, the hook clicking each time she advanced.

I watched, my eyes skirting from the movie theater to the freeway to Madeleine, my breathing ragged. When she stopped more than halfway to the top, we all leaned toward the pole, as if getting closer would help somehow.

"Are you okay?" CindeeRae's theater voice was swallowed by the sound of traffic. But Madeleine must have still heard, because she looked down and called back, "Just taking a break."

I held my breath until Madeleine pulled herself higher. As she did, her foot slipped from the rung and she jerked, the leash holding her in place as her lower body swayed in the air, her hands still clutching the ladder. Her legs swung wildly as she tried to regain her footing. I laced the extra leash around my waist and began to follow her.

"Don't." March grabbed my arm, but I shook him free and scrambled up the thin metal rungs, the bottoms of my shoes feeling slippery.

I could tell that Madeleine had been able to secure her hold on the ladder again. But she looked frozen up there.

"Are you okay?" I asked when I got close enough to see her face. Her eyes were closed, and it looked like she was whispering to herself.

"Not really." She gripped a rung with one hand and hugged the pole with the other. I heard her take a ragged breath. "I'm stuck. I can't go up or down."

I thought about calling our parents or even the police. But now that I had stopped, I wasn't sure I could move anymore either.

"Let's go down together," I said. "One step at a time. We have the leashes. We'll be fine." If I hadn't been terrified, I might have laughed hysterically at the idea that *any* of this was fine.

I could hear Madeleine breathing deeply, and just when I was about ready to repeat myself, she said, "But we're so close."

Seriously?

I heard clicking and looked up to see Madeleine move closer to the billboard. I grumbled and climbed behind her.

She finally reached the platform, pulled herself to safety, and collapsed onto her back. I followed until I was seated on the platform next to her.

Tentatively positioning herself within sight of the billboard, Madeleine removed the phone from her pocket and began taking pictures of the graffiti.

From close up I could finally see what had been sprayed over Blood Eagle's face. The outline of the baby Blood Eagle from the mural on the Super Pickle hovered over the billboard like a ghost. It was Blood Eagle's redesign, the one that had been published by Phoenix Rising and gotten so popular. Next to the image were the initials *CR*.

"*Blood Eagle: Origin of Deceit*," I muttered as I read the billboard again. Was the vandal trying to tell the world that not only had Marty Cavalier used Claudia Reed's character for the Blood Eagle comic, but he had also stolen her idea for the redesign?

"Let's hurry and get down," Madeleine said, dropping the phone back into her pocket and scooting toward the ladder.

I looked down to see March and CindeeRae pacing around the billboard post, small and squat as LEGO people. Everything I had eaten for dinner sloshed in my stomach. "I don't know if I can do this," I said.

"Yes, you can," Madeleine said, like she was coaching me from a soccer huddle. "Go."

I imagined we were climbing down from March's tree house and kept my eyes skyward as I lowered myself, rung by rung. My heart pounded in my ears. When we reached the ground, I dropped to my knees and patted the grass gratefully.

"Phew," Madeleine said. She pulled her hair from the tight ponytail and shook it out, smiling, her cheeks pink.

"That was the stupidest thing we've ever done," I said, accepting her hand to pull me back up.

CindeeRae yelled, "Called it," and yanked us all into a big group hug.

We shivered in our huddle under the freeway lights until March pulled back and asked, "Well, was it worth it?"

Madeleine bounced on her heels. "We just cracked our case."

CHAPTER THIRTY-THREE

March looked from me to Madeleine as we stood beneath the billboard. "How did we crack the case?" he asked. "What did you see?"

"A picture of the redesigned Blood Eagle with the initials *CR*," I said.

March shrugged. "What does that mean?"

Madeleine, still jittery with adrenaline, blurted, "Marty Cavalier got the idea for Blood Eagle from the Dark Writer artist, Claudia Reed." She went on in a rush. "They both owned Relic Comics, and Marty used that character when he created Blood Eagle for Phoenix Rising. That's why his name is in the credits for both comics."

"Wait a minute," CindeeRae interrupted. "What are you talking about?"

Madeleine went on as if she hadn't heard the question. "But the original Blood Eagle wasn't that popular. So Marty redesigned it, and the comic became super famous and now it even has a movie. Except, it seems like Claudia Reed—CR—is connected to the redesign, at least according to the vandal. Maybe she was even the one who *really* designed the character. Marty stole everything from her! It's obvious he betrayed her, and now she's exacting her revenge. *She's* our vandal."

Madeleine was making a huge leap without enough clues, but I had to admit, Claudia Reed was currently our biggest suspect.

"How do you know all this?" March asked, crossing his arms.

I gave Madeleine a look, silently willing her not to reveal our secret library mission, which I knew would divide the team even more. But she kept going. "Kazu and I studied the front pages from each comic and figured it all out. Well, with a little help from Mrs. Davis. She was the one who reminded us that Marty and Claudia were co-owners of Relic Comics—they created Dark Writer together. But her name wasn't listed in Blood Eagle, even though she was the one who had drawn the shadowy hero in that first issue."

CindeeRae and March exchanged cloudy looks, and then March spun on his heels and stomped back up the embankment.

"Hey," Madeleine called after him. "Where are you going?"

"Does it matter?" March asked as we scrambled to keep up with him. "You two don't need us! You've been running your own operations the whole time."

"You had given up anyway," I snapped back, my lava anger from the night of my parents' last fight swelling in my chest. He was the one who had decided we didn't have enough clues to do anything else. "You didn't even want to be on the case anymore."

"Not with you." March glared at me before turning his icy gaze on Madeleine. "Or you."

"Whatever!" Her voice sounded like old, bully Madeleine. "We don't need you anyway. We've practically solved the case on our own."

She walked away and left me standing there, shifting from one foot to the other. The air seemed to thicken around us. Finally, when no one said anything, I turned away from March and CindeeRae to catch up with Madeleine.

● ● ●

On Monday morning, the doorbell rang, and I ran downstairs to find Officer Rhodes standing in our entryway talking to Baa-chan.

"Come in," I heard her say as she led him into the kitchen. I trailed after them. "Would you like a cup of tea?"

"No, thanks," he said. "I was hoping to ask Kazuko a few questions."

"Kazuko?" Baa-chan said. "This Kazuko?" She nodded to me, as if we were surrounded by Kazukos.

"The one and only." Officer Rhodes's voice was sickly sweet. He sat down at one of the barstools at the counter and patted the seat next to him. I sat down.

His eyes locked on mine. "We had a few people call in last night to report some kids climbing a billboard—the same billboard that was targeted by our vandal, as a matter of fact."

I nodded, a knot in my throat making it impossible to say anything.

"The descriptions of these kids reminded me of someone." Officer Rhodes straightened his police jacket. "Any guesses who that someone might be?"

I shrugged, my heart slamming against my chest.

"Your little bicycle gang," he said. "You, March, CindeeRae, and that Maddie girl."

"Madeleine," I corrected.

"Oh no," Baa-chan interrupted. "Kazuko and her friends were at the movies last night."

Officer Rhodes's eyes slid from Baa-chan to me. "Really? Because *this* billboard happens to be right next to a movie theater." I pressed my lips together and didn't say anything. He couldn't make me answer his questions without a lawyer present. Or something like that.

Baa-chan puffed her chest out, walked from behind the kitchen counter, and stood beside me. I could feel the heat of her body, and I leaned into her. She hooked an arm around my shoulder and said, "I think it's time for you to go, Officer . . ."

"Rhodes," he finished.

"Officer Rhodes," she echoed. Baa-chan was small, but in that moment she seemed to fill the entire room.

"Of course. Thank you for your time." Officer Rhodes stopped on the front stoop, blocking the door with one foot in case Baa-chan decided to slam it on him. "We just worry about these kids getting themselves hurt or in trouble."

He finally stepped away and Baa-chan shut the door. Officer Rhodes got in his car and drove away, all while Baa-chan stood in our entryway, silently watching him. I let out a sigh of relief. She knew we had been studying the heaven spot at our last team meeting, and she still hadn't given me up. No one had stood up for me in a long time.

I was just about ready to hug her around the waist when she met me with her sharp gaze. "What were you thinking?"

"What do you mean?" I asked, although I knew exactly what she meant.

"Did you climb that billboard?" She shifted forward, and even though Baa-chan was only a few inches taller than me, it felt like her anger blocked the sun.

"I wasn't going to go," I whispered. "But then Madeleine slipped, so I followed her up." I only realized how bad that sounded after the words had fallen out of my mouth.

"You could be in the hospital right now, Kazuko!" It was one of the first times since she had gotten here that she had used my full name, instead of calling me Kazu-chan.

"But it was the only way to get the clue," I said.

"Is that more important than your safety?" she asked. "*Nothing* is more important than your safety. You're lucky I didn't turn you in to that policeman."

Baa-chan's voice was thick with disappointment; it reminded me of Mom's lectures. But with Mom and Dad so distracted they might as well be in the Bahamas, Baa-chan was the only one who felt like home right now. And I had messed it all up.

"You're grounded from friends this week." She grabbed my backpack from the floor and pushed it into my arms. "Now hurry or you'll miss the bus."

Genki whimpered as Baa-chan opened the door for me, shutting it behind me without saying good-bye.

CHAPTER THIRTY-FOUR

E ven though I was grounded, Madeleine and I continued to secretly search for the practice site after my paper route that week. We had decided to look beyond March's original scope of West Highland, opting to case out the areas surrounding the vandal's very first hit at Mile High Comics.

By Friday, we only had one more area to investigate. And, aside from a few random tags and swatches of graffiti, we hadn't seen anything that looked like our vandal's work in the three weeks we'd been searching.

The early morning quiet wasn't helping my spirits either. I had too much time to think about March refusing to sit next to me on the bus and Baa-chan walking around the house all quiet and cold. And without any leads on Mom's case, I was starting to feel like I'd never understand why she wasn't getting better.

As we rounded the second of the four blocks, I swerved into a dark alley between some boxy buildings and walked my bike toward the dumpster halfway down. For a minute, I considered telling Madeleine what I'd overheard Mom say about me being a leftover child. But my cheeks burned remembering that moment, and I realized I was afraid to admit it had even happened at all. There was a part of me that felt like saying it aloud would make it true. Then I would never get Mom back.

"What's that?" Madeleine asked. She pointed at a small neighborhood park across the street, closed in on one side by an ivy-covered fence.

"A park," I said as I walked my bike back to her. "Why?"

"Look at the climbing wall," she said.

In the far corner, a wide climbing wall stood, its backside up against the fence. Along the top edge, I could see trickles of black and orange, as if paint had accidentally dripped from the other side.

"Let's check it out." I got back on my bike and followed Madeleine across the street.

We wove our way through the park, riding on the grass and around the playground until we reached the climbing wall. It was the color of charcoal and looked like it was made from real rock, covered with colorful handholds. Laying our bikes on the ground, we slowly walked to the other side.

And gasped.

Covering the back surface, where all the handholds had been meticulously removed, was the image of Dark Writer. He was larger than life, with his arms outspread, and he was holding an oversize birdcage in one hand with a phoenix flapping its wings inside, red and orange feathers floating like leaves to the ground. Sprayed across the top of the wall in orange paint outlined in black was the phrase: YOU'RE FINISHED, PR.

"Whoa," I breathed.

I could hear birds chirping as the sun crept over the horizon, darkened by storm clouds. Madeleine's breath was as jagged as my own, and I knew she had just caught sight of the same thing I had.

Inside the birdcage, in the corner the phoenix seemed to be trying to flee, was a little black cartoon bomb. Its fuse was lit.

"Whoa is right," she echoed. "We found it. We found the practice site."

And a lot more than that.

Wordlessly, Madeleine took pictures of the wall before we left on our bikes, the wind the only sound swirling around us.

• • •

No matter how upset CindeeRae and March might be with us, we needed to have an emergency meeting, stat. Finding this newest clue at the practice site that morning had escalated the case to a Code Red, and we needed to talk about next steps.

Madeleine agreed to find CindeeRae at school that morning and meet March and me at the bus drop.

But approaching March was more difficult than I expected, since he continued to ignore me. When we reached Lincoln Elementary, I followed him off the bus.

"Can we please talk?" I whispered.

Before he could answer, Madeline and CindeeRae appeared. March shook his head and tried to step around them. "No way," he said under his breath.

"Please," I said. "We found the practice site, and you were right. It might be our best chance at finally cracking this case."

It seemed like everything was falling apart, and I knew that bringing the team back together might be the only way to save the case and catch our vandal. And even more important, it might be the only way to save our friendship.

He didn't meet my eyes, but he looked at CindeeRae, who shrugged and said, "We might as well see what it looks like."

We grabbed a bench on the playground, where Madeleine, CindeeRae, and I sat. March stood back, eyeing us suspiciously. He had every right to feel betrayed. If he and CindeeRae had gone on secret missions without me, I would have been spit angry, too.

"I'm sorry," I said. "We shouldn't have gone off on our own. We're a team, and a team works together."

Madeleine sighed, looking at her lap. "I'm really sorry about what I said at the billboard." She fiddled with her phone, flipping it over and over in her hands before she finally looked up and met March's gaze. "It wasn't fair for us to start our own investigations without letting you and CindeeRae know. In soccer, if you see the opportunity to make a play, you take it because there's no time for a huddle. I'm starting to learn that's not how it works with friends."

March stood silent, shifting his weight from one foot to the other. Finally, he nodded slowly before lowering himself onto the bench next to CindeeRae.

The four of us leaned together, shoulder to shoulder as we scrolled through the practice-site pictures on my SleuthPad. Kids ran across the playground, their squeals and laughter filling the air.

"I can't believe you found it," CindeeRae whispered.

"Wait." March snatched the SleuthPad from my hands, and I braced myself for an anxious discussion about the graffiti bomb in the mural. "Is that a different tag?" He pointed at the bottom corner of the screen.

Madeleine and I exchanged looks. A different tag? I

pulled the SleuthPad back and held it closer. There, in the corner of the picture, was a pile of feathers, most of them red. But on top, in a shade of orange that was difficult to tell apart from the rest, was a tag. Not the Dark Writer tag we were used to seeing, but something different. Two letters: ZC.

"Wait," CindeeRae broke the silence. "What does ZC stand for? Didn't you say Claudia Reed was the vandal? I mean, Marty Cavalier stole the Blood Eagle character from her."

"It's not Claudia," March said. When we all turned to stare at him, he shrugged. "I've been doing a little investigating of my own since the billboard incident."

"And?" Madeleine pressed.

"Claudia died last year. Cancer."

The anxious flutter in my chest at the thought of uncovering a case-cracking lead froze tight and dropped like a cold anchor to my stomach. Madeleine and I were certain we had cracked the case. Marty had betrayed Claudia, and she was exacting her revenge. It had all made sense. How could we be *this* close and not have one suspect?

Madeleine leaned back on the bench, hard.

CindeeRae shrugged. "That sucks."

I sighed, trying to rally before the entire team gave up. "Our first priority is trying to track down a suspect," I said. "But in the meantime, we need to monitor Phoenix Rising to make sure the vandal doesn't bomb the place before we get enough information for the police to stop it."

"How do we do that?" CindeeRae asked, and I was relieved to hear her say *we*. This case was definitely bigger than just Madeleine and me.

"Yeah, March," I said. "How do we do that?"

"I'll think about it," he said. "And get back to you."

I pressed my lips together, reminding myself that if March hadn't taken the time to discover Claudia's death, Madeleine and I would have spent even more time tracking down a lead that didn't even exist.

"But what about the bomb?" CindeeRae finally addressed what we thought would be the most important detail about the practice site. "Obviously our vandal is targeting Phoenix Rising next, and if we wait too long, he'll strike. And *that* hit will require more than a couple gallons of paint to fix."

"Well." Madeleine had leaned forward again, thinking. "Our vandal is still planning to paint the bomb mural somewhere, so there will be no big boom until after that, right? Which means more time to gather clues."

"Okay," I said. "I'm in."

"Me too," CindeeRae said. "But we need to tell the police as soon as the vandal paints the bomb mural."

March stared into his lap, considering.

"So?" I asked him. If our team operated by majority vote, he was outnumbered. But without his help, we might not be able to track down the information we needed.

March finally looked up, nodding. "I'm in, too."

CHAPTER THIRTY-FIVE

Since I was grounded, I brought my art project home and worked on it Saturday after dinner, gluing my cutouts to a foam board.

Dad ducked his head into the dining room to wink at me. "Art club must be going well," he said.

Baa-chan had just lit some incense next to O-jizō-sama and looked from Dad to me. Something about her expression made it clear that Dad didn't know about the billboard or that she had grounded me.

I turned back to Dad and smiled. "Yeah," I answered. "I actually love it."

"Keep up the good work," he said, giving me a cheesy thumbs-up as he left.

Baa-chan waved the match she had used to light

the incense, the flame disappearing, and walked into the dining room, where I was sitting. She slowed as she neared the table and then stopped. We hadn't spoken much since she had found out I climbed the billboard, and I wasn't sure how to get things back to the way they used to be.

"That looks really good, Kazu-chan." She nodded at the foam board. "Jōzu!"

"Thanks," I said, grateful that she was at least talking to me again.

As she busied herself in the kitchen, I continued to work on my project, waiting for the work to loosen the knot in my chest, the way it had when we did shodō. But I couldn't help but think about how disappointed Baa-chan had been with me.

I took deep breaths and focused on arranging the images. I wanted the backdrop to remind me of the feelings I had when looking at our vandal's murals or Baa-chan's canvas. The classical musical playing from my SleuthPad reminded me of art club, and soon the room faded away as I pasted together something that had never existed before. It was only when I heard Mom announce an outing with friends that I remembered where I was and looked up.

My eyes darted from Baa-chan to Dad, who had come back into the dining room. They both managed weird half smiles, like Mom had said she was going paragliding or shark fishing. I tried to stop my heart from shooting happy fireworks across my chest, reminding myself that last time she apparently hadn't even backed out of the driveway. All that progress I thought she had been making was pretend.

I stood and watched Mom pull out and drive away, Dad hovering behind me for a minute before he grabbed the newspaper and went downstairs.

Baa-chan continued to wash the dishes, and I sat down in the living room. Genki curled around my feet as I watched the last of the incense stick collapse into ashes next to O-jizō-sama.

"Can I sit next to you and knit my scarf?" Baa-chan still had a hand towel tossed over one shoulder and her temperature scarf clutched in her hands.

I got up to scoot over, but she sat down and patted her lap, and I readjusted to rest my head on her legs instead. The gesture felt like a call for a truce. I took a deep breath, and relief spread through my whole body. So many things in my life were broken, but my relationship with Baa-chan wasn't, and that seemed to make everything else feel a little bit better.

The scarf cascaded from her busy fingers, creating a blue, green, and yellow rainbow that fell over my face like a veil. As her needles clicked, I found my breath syncing with the sound.

"I'm sorry, Baa-chan," I finally said. "You were right.

Climbing the billboard was dangerous, and we shouldn't have done it."

Her knitting needles slowed for a beat, and I braced myself for a lecture. Instead, she picked up the pace and said, "You are very important to me, Kazu-chan. I would have been so sad if you had gotten hurt. And I can't begin to imagine how devastated your parents would have been if you had fallen." The temperature scarf continued its puppet dance, and I thought she was done talking. Then she said, "Promise me you won't do anything like that again."

I extended my hand toward her, pinkie outstretched. "I promise."

Baa-chan hooked my pinkie with her own and kissed the thumb-side of her hand.

I settled back onto her lap, staring at the serene expression on O-jizō-sama's face through the gaps in the temperature scarf, when something about the stone statue jolted me wide-awake. Baa-chan had shipped it from Japan especially for Mom. Something about O-jizō-sama was supposed to make her feel better. The biggest clue in the whole case had been sitting in our living room almost the entire time.

I snapped upright, jostling Baa-chan and her work. "I'm going to bed," I said so quickly it sounded like one word.

"Okay," she said, studying me as I grabbed my

SleuthPad from the dining room table and headed up the stairs. "O-yasumi-nasai."

"Good night, Baa-chan!" I beamed as Genki followed me to my room, certain I was minutes away from busting Mom's case wide open.

● ● ●

I ducked under my covers with my SleuthPad, waiting for Genki to tunnel in next to me. When we were finally settled, I opened up a browser window and typed *O-jizō-sama* in the search bar. The light from my screen glowed under my pink blanket as I clicked through search results.

O-jizō-sama was more than a Japanese lawn ornament. The statue represented a Buddhist deity that looked out for babies who had died young, or before they were even born. Parents and other family members dressed O-jizō-sama in bibs, scarves, and hats, hoping to convince him to carry their lost baby into the afterlife.

I let my SleuthPad fall onto my bed as I thought about what I had just read, my blanket tent going dark. One of the doctors in Mom's phone had been Dr. Slade, an obstetrician: a baby doctor. It had been almost twelve years since I had been born, so I thought the doctor Mom had been visiting before she had gotten sick couldn't possibly be Dr. Slade. But what if I was wrong?

I remembered what Mom had said, what had hurt to hear more than anything else ever: *I can't even manage to parent the child I have left.* Why would I be left when there had never been any other children?

My body turned cold as all the clues clicked into place. Mom had been *pregnant*. But then she must have lost the baby and gotten heartsick. Baa-chan had gotten her O-jizō-sama to help her grieve.

Case solved.

Genki began to whimper, and I realized that hot tears stung my cheeks. Mom was sad because my little baby brother or sister had died before they could even be born. My stomach swirled with emotions, like a washing machine packed to bursting. I couldn't even understand what I felt: a mixture of sadness, anger, and even a little relief. It was more than I could feel all at once, so I curled into a ball and let Genki nuzzle into me as I rocked myself to sleep.

CHAPTER THIRTY-SIX

I should have been happy to solve Mom's case. Not only had I found out why she was sad, but I had made up with Baa-chan and was no longer grounded. But instead I felt like I was walking around in metal armor, my feet dragging as I moved through the house.

When I couldn't stand it anymore, I rode my bike to March's on Sunday afternoon. His oldest sister, Maggie, walked me through the living room and into the back-yard, pointing me toward the tree house. The sun shone through the new green leaves, creating a shimmering canopy above the wooden retreat. Birds sang on the branches, reminding me of the aviary at the zoo.

I climbed the tree house ladder. "March? Are you up here?"

He didn't answer until I had reached the landing, yelling, "Come in."

I sat on an upside-down bucket, the hard plastic digging into my legs through the fleece blanket. March sat opposite me, the copies of internet research fanning out on the wall behind him, more than double what had been there for our last meeting. Even though he hadn't been involved in any field missions last week, he had obviously continued to research the case.

"So, what else did you find out?" I nodded at the new information, embarrassed that I had ever thought March couldn't uncover more than Madeleine and me.

"A lot of it confirms what you and Madeleine found." He shrugged. "Marty Cavalier and Claudia Reed started Relic Comics in college. It was a small side business. They were good friends, both students in the art program. Dark Writer and Calypso Robot were the only comics they made there. Neither did well."

"Then what happened?" I studied the picture from the practice site, blown up so that bomb in the back corner of the birdcage was easy to see, the fuse lit and flame close to the end.

"They graduated and Marty started his own publishing company here in Denver—Phoenix Rising," March said. "I couldn't find anything on why they let Relic Comics die. Claudia got married to a guy named Max Carson and worked as a graphic designer at a local marketing company for years. She did freelance artwork for comics on the side but never anything as big as Blood Eagle."

"She didn't sue Marty or anything?" I asked. "For stealing the Blood Eagle design?"

"Not that I could see," March said. "But Blood Eagle has only been super popular for the last five years or so, after PR rebranded the hero. About that same time Claudia's husband died and she had to take care of her stepdaughters. A couple of years later, Blood Eagle got the big movie deal and the rest is history."

A crackling silence settled in the tree house, and I brushed off my pants so that I had something to do with my hands. I looked up and met March's eyes. "Did you really mean it when you said you didn't want to work on this case with me?"

I thought of how hard it must have been for Madeleine to lose her best friend, and I realized how tense things had been between March and me since practically the beginning of this case. We both seemed to have changed, me becoming closer to Madeleine, and him not wanting to be involved in this investigation much anymore.

March avoided my eyes and plugged the Christmas lights into the long extension cord that snaked down the tree trunk and through the backyard. The ceiling burst into color, a low-hanging red light flashing against his cheek. "It just feels like everything is different. You're all doing other things. CindeeRae has her play, and you and Madeleine have art club. All I have is computers and comic books."

"It's okay if we like different things," I said. "We're still part of the same team."

March looked at the floor. "Ever since Owen started talking about closing the Super Pickle, it's all I can think about. I thought if I could solve this case, it would fix everything. But I can never figure anything out—you solve everything first. And there are so many people on the team now that it doesn't matter whether or not I'm there."

I looked around the tree house, covered with clues and timelines. "You just figured out even more than Madeleine and I had with Mrs. Davis."

"Anyone can search the internet." He sat on his bucket, and it skidded back a few inches before it hit the wall.

"Come on, March," I said. "You're a genius. We'd all be totally lost if the case required any hacking."

"Maybe." He began shuffling all his papers together and slid them into his notebook. "But so far, you and Madeleine act like you have everything figured out."

I didn't say anything, remembering the way we had taken off to document the mural at Comic Relief before the store owners painted over it. Even then, I knew the operation would upset March. And then sneaking off to work with Mrs. Davis on more case research, lying about where we were going and what we were doing.

"But then I realized that maybe it doesn't matter after all." March looked out the window, away from me. "Even with all the work we've done to catch the vandal, Owen might still close his store."

That was exactly how I had felt about my Mom's case—that there couldn't possibly be anything more important than finding out what was wrong. And now that I had solved it, nothing had changed; she was still sad. For the first time, I told March about how Mom had been in bed for nearly a month, that Baa-chan had come to help take care of us, and that I had just found out Mom had lost her baby.

"Why didn't you tell me?" he asked when I was done, finally meeting my eyes.

I shrugged. "I guess I was afraid of finding out what was wrong—so it was hard to talk about it. Plus, I knew that you had your own things to worry about."

"I didn't even notice," he said. "I'm sorry I wasn't a very good friend."

"Neither was I," I admitted. "We were both a little distracted."

I let the silence settle around us. Finally, I said, "So,

what do we do about our case? We've chased down our leads and still don't have a suspect."

He smiled. "I did a little digging and discovered that Phoenix Rising has a security system." When I raised my eyebrows in confusion, he explained. "If we hack into it, we'll at least be able to see if our vandal does anything fishy and notify the police before he has a chance to bomb the publishing company."

I smiled back. My best friend and techie guru extraordinaire, March Winters, would end up hacking after all.

CHAPTER THIRTY-SEVEN

I got up an hour earlier to do the route so we'd have plenty of time to hack the camera at Phoenix Rising before school started that Monday. It had rained the night before, and the sky was still overcast, a rumbling, deep purple.

We dropped our bikes on the sidewalk in front of the old warehouse that had been repurposed for the comic book publisher. PHOENIX RISING hung across the top of the building in black letters, while a neon sign of the red-and-orange phoenix logo flashed in the window.

The warehouse was surrounded by an empty parking lot in a neighborhood of big buildings just like this one. Performing this operation at night would have provided better cover but would have also been a violation of multiple rules from four different households. Not that we were exemplary citizens in the first place, but I didn't want to disappoint Baa-chan with another risky night mission. So we'd have to be slick not to get caught hacking this camera in the open.

Of course, there was also the little problem of meddling in an open investigation and possibly, probably, breaking the law, but we had decided that this option was like an undercover security mission: We would protect Phoenix Rising while preventing our vandal from committing a dangerous crime. Win, win, right?

We all moved to the edge of the building, where we huddled behind the corner. March powered on his sister Maggie's iPad and tapped away at the screen while the rest of us waited, the breath from our mouths hanging in the air like little clouds. Maggie, the oldest Winters kid, was a master hacker; she had already been awarded a full-ride scholarship for MIT that fall. Her iPad was certain to be loaded with all the hacking software March could ever need.

"First I have to hack into their network." March typed away while Madeleine, CindeeRae, and I stood watching.

Suddenly, he looked away from the screen, his fingers still.

"What?" CindeeRae squeaked, her eyes skittering around us. "There's no time for breaks. Get hacking!"

"I know, I know." March turned his attention back to the iPad, his brain practically humming. "I just needed to run this program that captures the PMKID and dumps it into a file, which I'll convert into a harsh format . . ." He looked up to see our blank faces. "Never mind. I'm just running some apps to get their Wi-Fi password."

CindeeRae paced while March worked, the gravel in the parking lot crunching beneath her sneakers. Once March hacked into Phoenix Rising's network, we'd be able to stream all the security footage to his computer, my SleuthPad, or Madeleine's iPhone. March could even trigger an alert that would sound as soon as it caught anything, so we could call the police before our vandal broke into the building. March insisted on that last part.

"How much longer?" I asked as the sky got lighter and more cars started to appear in the street outside the parking lot.

"About five minutes," March said, plucking away at the iPad.

Madeleine began pacing opposite CindeeRae. Every few steps, their paths would cross before they spun around and walked toward each other again. After a few rotations, they began high-fiving each time they passed.

"I'm almost done . . ." March began as a car pulled into the parking lot next to the warehouse steps.

CindeeRae gasped, and the three of us ducked

behind the building, leaving March hacking his little heart out against the brick wall.

As we peeked around the corner, he slunk back to us, hissing, "Why didn't you warn me?!"

"Maybe they're lost," Madeleine whispered.

The sound of a slamming door echoed in the alley. Without warning, Madeleine walked toward the sound.

"What are you doing?" CindeeRae muttered after her.

Madeleine held up a hand in response before getting on her knees to crawl toward the front steps. She dropped out of sight for a few seconds, and my heart pounded as I imagined someone grabbing her arm and calling the police.

Moments later, she rushed back to where we waited and said, "He went inside."

"We've got to get out of here," CindeeRae said, and I looked around for a possible escape route.

"But I'm not done yet!" March waved the iPad at us.

As I studied the other end of the alley, I noticed the flashing light above the loading dock where one of PR's security cameras hung. "Look," I said, pointing with a shaky finger. "They'll be able to see us."

"Not if I can help it." March beamed as he went back to work on the iPad. "Once I'm in, I'll delete that part of the feed."

The four of us scrunched a little lower, flattening ourselves against the back wall when we heard footsteps.

"We need to hide," I said, motioning toward the dumpster butted up against the backside of the building. "In there."

Following CindeeRae, we skittered to the yellow dumpster. Madeleine shoved her phone into her back pocket and lifted the lid while the rest of us barreled inside, landing on broken-down cardboard boxes and packing peanuts. I let out a sigh of relief that it wasn't full of old takeout containers and coffee grounds. Once March, CindeeRae, and I were inside, March stood to hold the lid up while Madeleine leaped to the edge like a real athlete. She tumbled in and we slowly closed the dumpster, dropping us into darkness.

I bumped March with my shoulder. "Are you done yet?"

"Almost." The screen's reflection caught his face in an eerie glow.

The footsteps echoed in the alley, and March turned the iPad upside down, cutting all light. Our breath seemed to thunder in the dumpster as we waited. The footsteps hammered closer, and Madeleine grabbed my hand and squeezed hard, cutting the circulation to my fingers. And then, silence. Our breathing stopped, and I could feel the pressure build as my lungs ached. March was the first to inhale, and I was certain the whole neighborhood could hear the sudden intake of air.

The footsteps moved away at a speedy clip, and the four of us gasped in relief.

Madeleine's voice cut through the darkness. "We've got to get out of here. Fast."

"What about our bikes?" CindeeRae asked.

March was already tapping away at the screen again, while Madeleine lifted the dumpster's lid a crack to peek outside. "We should get the bikes and bring them back here for a quick getaway."

"What?" CindeeRae was clearly not on board with this plan.

"She's right," I said. "They might call the police, and if our bikes are still out there, we'll be in big trouble."

Leaving March to hack away in the dumpster, the three of us snuck around the other side of the building, away from the security camera. When we peered at the front of Phoenix Rising, the car was still parked in front, the engine running. I eyed our four bikes, lying on the cement.

"Okay," I said. "On the count of three, we grab them."

"Wait, wait, wait." CindeeRae pulled on my shoulder with her hand. "We don't even know where that guy is."

"We can't wait to find out," I said, my teeth clenched.

No one said anything, so I began to count. "One. Two. Three!"

We ran out wildly, focusing on the bikes where the sidewalk and walkway met. As I reached for the handlebars of my bike, a man ran from the building and shouted, "What are you kids doing?"

He sounded more curious than upset. We paused to

glance at him, the skin on the back of my neck prickling. *Marty Cavalier.* After all that time studying the article in the *Denver Accolade* about Relic Comics, I recognized him immediately. He was tall and lean, his thick black hair slick and tight on his head. He stood like an action figure—arms stiff and held away from his body.

I grabbed my bike and yanked it upright, realizing that March would need his, too. CindeeRae and Madeleine both pulled their cruisers up and got on their bikes in one jerky movement, lurching toward the backside of the building.

"What . . ." the man muttered to himself, and ran down the steps toward me, pumping his arms at his sides. "What are you doing here?" His voice deepened, with an I-mean-business edge.

I picked up March's bike, holding one of his handlebars in one hand and one of mine in the other, trying to run away as they wobbled precariously on either side of me. Cavalier's shoes slapped the pavement behind me as I darted around the building. March tumbled from the dumpster just as I reached him.

We clambered onto our bikes and followed CindeeRae and Madeleine from the scene, fast as we could, iPads bouncing in my basket. As we sped away, cool wind whipping at my hair, I felt relief flood my body. *Except . . .* My stomach cramped with the realization. Even if March had erased us from Phoenix Rising's security feed, Marty Cavalier had just seen our faces.

CHAPTER THIRTY-EIGHT

Baa-chan had started packing, loading up her extra suitcase with all the American goodies she wanted to take back to Japan for Jii-chan and her friends. So while we got to keep all the tea cakes and gummy candies, ceramic rice bowls, washi paper, chopsticks, and Kewpie mayonnaise Baa-chan had brought for us, she was replacing it with bulk American cereal, phone cases for her friends, and a five-pound bag of Sour Patch Kids.

As she shuffled between the laundry room and the pantry, carrying armfuls of stuff back to her room, I sat at the kitchen counter eating my snack while Mom leaned against the sink, drinking tea. The sound of our swallowing filled the room.

A few weeks ago, I would've been happy to see Baa-chan pack, but now my stomach twisted at the thought of quiet afternoons without her. Mom would return to work at the museum on Monday, although she would be home after school. Still, I didn't believe things would ever be like they had been before she got the bedroom sickness. Before she lost the baby.

I thought that knowing what had caused Mom's sadness would help me fix it. But the knowing made *me* sad, too, and even a little angry that my parents hadn't told me. Then I remembered what Madeleine had said on the way home from ComiCanon, about how maybe Mom hadn't told me what was going on because I hadn't asked her. Maybe if I finally asked her, if we could talk about it together, things could at least get better?

I watched Mom drink the last of her tea, the cup balanced on the palm of her hand.

"Mom?" My heart thundered.

"Yes?" She looked up and met my eyes.

"Can I ask you something?" When I was in third grade, I had asked that question all the time. Mom had gotten frustrated and told me to just come out and ask what I wanted to in the first place. But this time, instead of looking annoyed, her face softened, and she pulled out a chair so she could sit next to me.

"What is it, Kazu?"

The question lodged in my throat. I coughed into my fist to make room for it. "Why didn't you tell me you were going to have a baby?"

"What?" Her face went white except for two red spots on her cheeks. "How did you know?"

"I did a little detecting," I said. "But when I figured out what the O-jizō-sama was, I finally understood."

"Of course my little detective would crack the case." Mom smiled weakly and released a long sigh. "I'm sorry that this has all been so mysterious to you. That's not fair."

I looked at the counter, the dappled design blurring into a big gray blob.

She cleared her throat and began. "After you were born, we wanted another baby, someone who could be your little brother or sister. When that didn't happen, we realized how lucky we were to have you. We were perfectly happy to move forward as a three-person family."

I looked at her and saw that her eyes were teary, too.

"So we were shocked when your father and I realized I was pregnant a few months ago," she said, drumming her fingertips on the counter. "It had been years since we had stopped trying, but we were both so excited to give you a baby sister." She scraped at a phantom spot on the counter.

"A sister?"

"Yes." She sniffled and looked up. "We had just found out and were about to tell you when I lost the baby. We were devastated. Baa-chan came to help."

I slumped in the seat and felt Genki lick my fingers.

"I'm so sorry, sweetie. We should have told you." She draped her arm over my shoulder and pulled me to her side, where I felt her heart thrum in my ear. "I wish I could go back and do everything differently. But after the miscarriage . . ."

Her voice broke, and I decided *miscarriage* was the stupiest word ever. It made it sound like Mom had been carrying the baby wrong, like it was her fault the pregnancy didn't last. As I inhaled, my chest ached like I was breathing in glass shards. I was going to be a big sister and never had a chance to know about it. And now I only knew because it wasn't going to happen.

Baa-chan had walked over and stood just inside the kitchen doorframe, watching me. I rubbed Genki's velvety ears between my fingers. Both Mom and Baa-chan waited for me to respond, but my chest heaved, and my breath came too quickly. I stood up. Genki jumped from the bench seat to follow me. "I'm going to my room, if that's okay," I finally said.

For the first time I could understand why Mom had spent so much time hiding from the world. When I shut the door to my room behind me, I wasn't sure I ever wanted to come out again.

● ● ●

The team gathered around our dining room table to figure out who ZC was. Baa-chan had just lit incense by O-jizō-sama, and the smell spread through the room. Genki sneezed as he pushed his way between the empty chairs to plop down beneath the table.

"Are you hungry for lunch yet?" Baa-chan asked as she passed through to the kitchen. It was a lazy Saturday morning, and through the window we could see Dad raking up all the winter garbage and carrying new plants to the flower bed I had cleared a few weeks ago.

"Not yet," I said. "But maybe later."

"Then I'll knit," she said, and went over to the window seat to work on the temperature scarf, which was looking long enough to wrap O-jizō-sama up like a mummy.

"What are we looking for?" CindeeRae didn't even wait for Baa-chan to leave the room before she started talking.

"Anyone close to Claudia who would want revenge on Marty for stealing Blood Eagle."

"Her parents are super old," March said, "and live in Florida."

"So," Madeleine said. "Not them."

"What about her stepdaughters?" I asked. "They're still around, right?"

"One was sixteen and the other was eleven when she died." March pushed the copy of Claudia Reed's obituary across the table so Madeleine and I could study it.

"Did she have any brothers or sisters?" CindeeRae asked, and March shook his head.

I ran my finger over the paragraph about the stepdaughters, stopping on the oldest one's name. "Guys," I said. "Claudia's stepdaughters are Zoey and Alexandra Carson."

"ZC," Madeleine whispered, and leaned over to read the paragraph with me. "Zoey Carson."

I woke up my SleuthPad and began a search, clicking on the first website displayed. My fingers tingled. "I found something," I said, scrolling down the screen. "A blog called Skater Queen. I think it's Zoey's."

"What's it say?" Madeleine asked, turning all her attention on me.

I turned the SleuthPad toward them. "I searched for *Zoey Carson* and *Denver*. This was the first thing to pop up."

"Whoa," CindeeRae said as she scrolled down the screen. "That's our skate park."

"I know," I said.

"And she's talking about her dad's death here."

Madeleine grabbed the SleuthPad and zoomed in on a picture of the Skater Queen's Vans, scuffed and torn, right next to a picture of a blurred tombstone. "And the death of her stepmom here."

"And this blog belongs to Claudia's stepdaughter?" CindeeRae asked.

"Obviously," I said. "I mean, each post is signed by ZC. That's Zoey, right?"

"It's got to be her!" Madeleine stopped on a frame from the original Blood Eagle comic and read to herself while the rest of us buzzed over our discovery.

"It's actually kinda cool," CindeeRae admitted. "And she's really good."

Madeleine interrupted, "Her mom died when she was a baby. And after losing her dad, she didn't deal with her stepmom's death very well. She was pulled out of school for a month, sent to a psychiatrist, threatened with some boot-camp wilderness program."

"That's horrible," I said. "She became an orphan at sixteen."

"She only bounced back when she came up with a plan to make sure her stepmom's greatest work would no longer be a secret." Madeleine passed the SleuthPad to CindeeRae, who had been straining to see the pictures. "She doesn't say what the *plan* was, but I'm guessing it's becoming Dark Writer."

"Huzzah!" March yelped from his seat and punched a fist into the air. "I can't believe we just found out who the vandal is."

I asked, "So, what next?"

CindeeRae said, "We call the police," as Madeleine said, "We confront her!"

Just then, Mom walked in. I hardly noticed her ironed clothes and straight hair. "Should I make you all lunch?" she asked.

CHAPTER THIRTY-NINE

We ate in silence, Madeleine picking away the crust on her grilled-cheese sandwich until there was hardly anything left to eat. March ate the apples like orange slices, leaving a smile of red peel on his plate, while CindeeRae wiped a milk mustache from her upper lip. Our eyes kept flicking to one another; I felt ready to burst from our big break.

"We should look for Zoey at the skate park," Madeleine finally whispered.

"Shhhhhhh," I said, eyeing Mom as she worked in the kitchen.

Once we had finished eating, we dumped our paper plates into the garbage and started to go outside. I stopped in the doorway. "Baa-chan, is it okay if we go to the park?"

Baa-chan's brows dropped low on her forehead, an unspoken complaint. "Ask your mother, Kazu-chan."

We hadn't really spoken since I had asked about the baby. While I understood why my parents hadn't told me, I hadn't yet been able to shake the weight on my heart. I turned to Mom and asked, "Can we?"

"Do you have the emergency phone?" she asked.

I patted my back pocket where the flip phone rested. She nodded, and I ran out of the house.

The four of us zoomed down the street on our bikes, our chains humming in the air as we sped along Honeysuckle toward the Denver Skate Park.

CindeeRae yelled over her shoulder as she led the way. "We should call the police!"

"We should stop yelling about it," Madeleine shouted back. We hadn't created any rules for this mission, but if we had, the first would have been to keep case information confidential, which included not blabbing in public.

"For the record," March yelled from behind me. "I agree with CindeeRae."

We rode the rest of the way in silence, the cards in March's spokes ticking like a clock.

● ● ●

The four of us sat cross-legged on a patch of grass in front of two skate park bowls. Kids flitted around us on roller skates, skateboards, scooters, and bikes, dipping in and out of the deeper dishes like professionals.

While we knew it was a long shot, we'd thought we'd check the skate park to see if we could find our Skater Queen. I imagined she would be speeding around, doing all sorts of tricks, her board snapping right back to her feet after every jump and flip like Thor's hammer.

March leaned forward. "I thought you said that once we found out who the vandal was, we'd call the police."

He was right. Now would be a good time to give Officer Rhodes all our information. But knowing that our vandal was Claudia Reed's stepdaughter, an orphaned teenager who was probably still sad about both her parents' deaths, made me feel bad for her. I mean, if we could convince her to turn herself in, she wouldn't be able to bomb Phoenix Rising and would get in less trouble.

I pulled the grass at my feet and made a little pile in front of me. "It's different now, knowing how upset she probably is. I mean, her stepmom died, and no one else knows that Claudia was the artist who created Blood Eagle, and probably the redesign, too."

"It doesn't matter how mad she is," March cut in. "It doesn't make what she did okay."

A kid on a scooter shot from one of the bowls and

nearly ran us over. CindeeRae dove out of his way dramatically, and we moved farther from the cement, still searching for a possible match for Zoey Carson.

"It doesn't make it okay." I thought about how upset Mom was that my baby sister had died, and how it made her act differently. "It just explains *why* she's doing it."

"She lives with her dad's brother now, right?" Madeleine asked. "It shouldn't take too long to find out where they live."

I looked at March again, putting on my humblest expression. "You could do some online investigating and find their address."

"Creepers." CindeeRae smirked. "You're talking about stalking."

"It's detecting, CR," Madeleine said. CindeeRae responded with a reluctant smile. "And once we get the address, we confront Zoey. Convince her not to bomb Phoenix Rising and maybe even turn herself in."

I thought about what *I* wanted to happen. While it was wrong for Zoey to vandalize all those comic book stores, was it any worse than what Marty had done?

"I agree with Madeleine," I said. "We should confront her. If she doesn't listen, *then* we tell the police."

"That sounds like a good plan," March agreed, meeting my smile with his own.

"So who tells the police?" CindeeRae asked, the wind blowing red curls into her face.

"We all can," March said. "We'll tell the police together."

"That's right," Madeleine agreed. "We're a team."

This whole crazy story sounded like it had come from a comic itself. But even comics had endings. We just had to make sure this case had an ending we could all live with.

CHAPTER FORTY

Madeleine and I hadn't been to art club in a couple weeks, and we were both anxious to finish our projects. Madeleine was now working on two different pieces. She buzzed with excitement as she unloaded things from her backpack and set them onto the table next to my picture-collage, which I was planning to embellish with acrylic paint.

Mr. Maximillian stood at the front of the class, already painting tropical flowers onto a thin sheet of wood propped against the whiteboard. The classical music carried through the room in soft waves, and I sat down, ready to relax and focus on my project.

Inspired by the piece Baa-chan had made for Mom, I had added cropped pictures of my own family over the backdrop of magazine cutouts and graffiti art. I dipped my brush in the red paint and, practicing on a paper towel, swept through the strokes for one of the kanji I wanted to include in my project.

Penny and Zannie erupted in laughter, standing at their easels in the back of the room. I watched them as they worked, Zannie using a paint knife to cut thick globs of colors onto her canvas.

Penny peered over Zannie's shoulder. "Why, Alexandra, what great masterpiece are you currently working on?" she asked in a dramatic British accent.

"Oh, just a little something for the Louvre," Zannie said, and Penny laughed with her again.

I turned back to my foam board, something about their conversation snagging in my brain. Dipping the brush in my water cup, I thought, *Alexandra*.

Alexandra Carson.

My heart thundered as I drew in a sharp breath. Digging my nails into Madeleine's arm, I whispered, "Code Red."

"Ow!" Madeleine pulled her arm away and snapped, "That hurts!"

"Sorry," I whispered, looking over my shoulder to make sure no one could overhear me. "But I just realized something *huge*!"

Madeleine followed my gaze and glanced over her shoulder, too, drawing the attention of both Zannie and

Penny. They stared back a second before looking at each other and bursting into laughter again.

We both snapped back in our seats.

I leaned into Madeleine and breathed in her ear, "Penny just called Zannie *Alexandra*. If Zannie is short for Alexandra, then her full name is . . ."

Madeleine gasped, frozen in her seat. "Alexandra Carson, Claudia's youngest stepdaughter!"

"What do we do?"

She shrugged, but my brain was already moving a mile a minute. If we told Zannie that Zoey was the vandal, maybe she could convince her sister to stop before Zoey got into real big trouble.

Madeleine smiled as if she had read my mind. "We confront Zannie instead," she finally said.

I nodded. "But how do we do that? I mean, how do we talk to her alone?"

Madeleine chewed on her bottom lip and then drew her phone from her back pocket. "We can't do anything yet. Not without talking to March and CindeeRae."

She was right. We both sat in silence, our projects splayed across the table. I dipped my brush into my water cup again, only this time to clean it. We wouldn't be finishing our projects today.

We excused ourselves to go to the bathroom, and Madeleine connected to March and CindeeRae in a group call. Madeleine held the phone in her cupped

263

hands, sound on speaker, and we both hovered over it as our voices echoed in the empty bathroom. We told them about our discovery, Madeleine and I tripping over each other's words as we asked what they thought about our plan to confront Zannie during art club.

"Do it!" March said. "Otherwise we have to wait until I find their address, which could take a while."

CindeeRae agreed, then asked, "How are you going to do it?"

"We're not sure," I said. "We have to talk to her alone, away from Penny."

March said, "Pass her a note. Tell her to meet you in the bathroom at three."

"Both of us?" Madeleine asked.

The clock on Madeleine's phone flashed 2:35, so we'd have to act fast.

"Just one of you," CindeeRae interrupted. "The other should make sure Penny doesn't get suspicious and come to investigate."

Madeleine nodded, considering. "Okay. Kazu will give Zannie the note, and I'll distract Penny."

"Let us know what happens," CindeeRae said just as her mom called for her in the background. "Gotta go."

March stayed on the line. "Guys?" he said, his voice low and secretive. "Thanks for calling."

Madeleine smiled. "You got it, boss."

We returned to our table in the art room. I ripped

a corner from a paper towel and scribbled in black ink, *Meet me in the bathroom at three.* I rolled it into a small scroll and stuffed it in my pocket.

"Let's go," I said.

Our chairs scraped against the floor as we stood. Following Madeleine, I meandered around our table and through the room, pretending to see what our classmates were working on. Finally, we made our way to the back, where Zannie and Penny now worked in silence.

"Wow, that's cool!" Madeleine said as she stood behind Penny, who stopped painting to stare at her suspiciously. Her picture was a creepy abstract of herself, the face cracked and distorted like she was looking into a broken mirror. "No, really. It's super cool."

In that moment, I pulled the note from my pocket and dropped it into an empty well in Zannie's paint palette. Her eyes dropped to the note and then back to me.

"You guys are weeeeeiiiiiiiiiird," Penny said, drawing out the last word until she practically ran out of air.

"We should get back to work," I said, stepping toward our table.

"Yep," Madeleine said. "We shoooouuuuld." She copied Penny and dragged out the sentence, leaving no doubt as to how weird we actually were.

We returned to our table and waited the agonizing thirteen minutes until three o'clock.

● ● ●

While I went to the bathroom, Madeleine stayed in the art room to watch Penny. I left five minutes early so that no one would be suspicious that Zannie and I were taking a bathroom break at the same time.

Pacing in front of the bathroom stalls, I rehearsed what I would say before Zannie arrived. I used big gestures as I detailed her sister's crimes and pleaded with her to stop Zoey from bombing Phoenix Rising. But when Zannie finally opened the bathroom door, all the words fell from my head, and I simply said, "Your sister is a vandal, and you need to stop her."

She scrunched up her face and said, "What are you talking about?"

"There's really no way you could have known," I said, trying to be sympathetic. "But your sister's been vandalizing comic book stores for months now because Marty Cavalier stole Blood Eagle from your stepmom. It's very complicated, but you've got to believe me when I say that if she doesn't stop, she's going to get in big trouble. Like colossal trouble. Like jailbird trouble." I took a deep breath.

"You're crazy." She took a step back like I had threatened her. "My sister wouldn't do anything like that."

"Grief makes you do crazy things." I thought of Mom

becoming a bedroom hermit for a month. "Believe me, I know."

"You don't know anything." Zannie's voice boomed in the bathroom, and she turned to wash her hands at the sink, even though she hadn't touched anything while we'd been there. Still, I watched swirls of blue and green water spin around the drain, before she turned the faucet off, ripped a paper towel from the dispenser, and left me there, her footfalls echoing in the bathroom long after she'd left.

CHAPTER FORTY-ONE

We had been so busy following the footage from Phoenix Rising's security camera that I had forgotten to check the paper for any more vandal hits.

CindeeRae waved today's copy of the newspaper at me as I walked in late to class. Mrs. Thomas narrowed her eyes in our direction, and CindeeRae folded the paper in half and slid it back into her desk. I slumped in my seat. Our failed mission with Zannie Carson the afternoon before made me uneasy, and it was looking more and more like we'd be unable to stop Zoey. Had we wasted all our time on this case, for nothing?

At lunch CindeeRae was so excited to talk about the article that she grabbed my hand and dragged me to the lunchroom, where we met March and Madeleine at our table. CindeeRae and March both started talking at the same time until Madeleine held up her hand and interrupted them. "Since March is leading this investigation, he should go first."

CindeeRae scowled at Madeleine before settling into her seat.

"I had to hack into Phoenix Rising's network in order to access their security camera," he said slowly, trying to drag out the suspense. "That means I have access to everything. Production files. Contracts. Everything. I realized that early this morning."

Even though she had argued for March's right to speak first, Madeleine looked bored already.

"So?" I said. "What did you find?"

"A file on Claudia," March said. "Contracts and correspondence from when she and Marty were partners. But the most recent thing in the file was the copy of an email she sent him after her husband died."

He looked at each of us meaningfully. Finally, CindeeRae yelled, "What did it say?"

"Before they closed Relic Comics, Claudia had already made the entire first volume of Blood Eagle, deciding it would do better if they softened the character. She proposed the redesign right before Marty backed out of their business. She said she had proof that Marty had stolen everything, but she wouldn't sue if he would just pay her for her work. Things were tight and she begged for his help. It wasn't the first email like that she'd sent. But it didn't look like he'd ever responded."

"UGH!" Madeleine said. "Marty is a horrible human."

"Totally," CindeeRae agreed.

Claudia must have been so desperate to send that email. I pushed my pizza quesadilla into the lunch trade-pile, my appetite fading as I imagined how disappointing it must have been to have her college friend and ex–business partner completely ignore her request.

"On the plus side," March said, "I also discovered where they keep future issues of Clarence the Betrayer."

"March!" CindeeRae used her shaming voice.

"I won't read them now." He ducked his head. "But maybe later? Like, after the vandal is arrested?"

"Why would she be arrested?" I asked, thinking back to all Zoey's posts about losing her father and stepmom. It had been a year since Claudia had died, and Zoey's most recent post was still sad and angry, like she was carrying around a heavy package she couldn't get rid of. Going to jail would only make things worse for Zoey.

"Duh," CindeeRae said. "Everything she's done so far is illegal, and planting a bomb is *super* illegal. She may never get out of jail for that one."

"But if we can stop her before the bomb—" My voice quavered a bit. "It won't be as bad."

"Is it time to talk about the newspaper article yet?" CindeeRae interrupted before anyone could respond. "The vandal—"

"Zoey," I corrected.

"Zoey," CindeeRae continued, "struck again last night, painting the same mural we found at the practice site on the Wells Fargo Center downtown." She pushed the local section toward us with the picture of Dark Writer holding the birdcage with the cowering phoenix on the double-domed entrance. Next to the mural *Return to ashes, PR* dripped down the glass in white spray paint.

Madeleine took a bite of her boloney sandwich and muttered with a full mouth, "That's not creepy at all."

It *was* super creepy. And while a part of me had been hoping our vandal wasn't capable of planting a bomb, this hit seemed to prove she might be.

We all sat in silence until CindeeRae muttered, "Yowza."

"It can't be long now," March said, lowering his voice, "before the b-o-m-b." He spelled it out, like anyone who might be eavesdropping was *that* bad at spelling.

CindeeRae nodded slowly. "We need to tell the police."

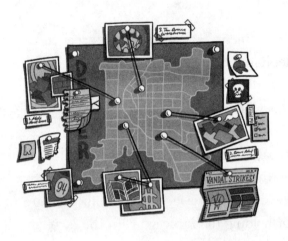

CHAPTER FORTY-TWO

After school that day, we all rode to the rock wall to see if Zoey had painted anything new. Maybe we were wrong and the bomb was metaphorical: a graffiti bomb. While March and CindeeRae wouldn't admit it, I knew they were curious to see the practice site in person. But when we walked to the backside of the climbing wall, we all stood with our jaws slack.

The mural had already been painted over, the dark gray spray paint leaving gashes of red and orange peeking through. Over the top, in thick white letters, read *Peace out, cupcakes.*

"Wait," CindeeRae asked. "Are *we* the cupcakes in this scenario?"

"Probably." I shrugged.

"She knows we're onto her," Madeleine said, shaking her head. "How does she know?"

"Zannie probably told Zoey that I confronted her," I said. I elbowed Madeleine and nodded at the wall, reminding her to take pictures. She slid her phone from her back pocket and got to work while the rest of us watched.

"When do you think she'll bomb Phoenix Rising?" CindeeRae asked.

March just shrugged.

"It seems like she timed all the other hits around the *Blood Eagle* movie release," I said. "Maybe there's an even bigger day she's building toward."

Madeleine stopped taking pictures to look at me. "You're right." She turned to March and CindeeRae. "She's totally right."

"So you think she'll plant the bomb on a specific day? Like a holiday or something?" CindeeRae asked, still staring at the word *cupcakes*.

"Maybe?" I said, although *holiday* wasn't exactly right.

"What other big dates are there?" March asked. We all fell silent, the cool breeze making the leaves above us shudder on their branches.

• • •

The four of us sat in the library the next day during lunch, watching Mrs. Davis prepare new books for shelving behind the checkout counter.

"It's time to officially close this case," March said. "Can everyone go to the police station tonight?"

We all looked wilted, like a bouquet of week-old flowers. Even though we had found our vandal, we hadn't been able to stop her, making this meeting completely unsatisfying.

"I have rehearsal tonight," CindeeRae said. "But I can go tomorrow."

"Me too," I said, and Madeleine nodded.

March sighed. "We'll hand all our case files over to Officer Rhodes so the police can stop Zoey from bombing Phoenix Rising."

March pushed a thick folder to the middle of the table, packed with all the notes that had been pinned to his tree house walls less than twenty-four hours ago. As he did, the door to the library clanged open, and Zannie walked in, her long dark hair disheveled, like she had just parachuted into school.

"That's Alexandra Carson," I mouthed to the group.

We all turned and watched as Zannie leaned over the counter to whisper something to Mrs. Davis. The librarian nodded as Zannie turned to go, shooting her a sad smile.

Just then, Zannie's head swung in our direction, her

eyes widening as she caught us watching her. She froze in place, holding her hands out like she was carrying an invisible dodgeball. It was so quiet, I thought I could hear myself blink. Then she darted from the library with another loud clang.

That's when Mrs. Davis noticed us and smiled.

"Well, hello, gang!" She walked to our table. "How did I miss you over here?"

Madeleine cleared her throat and said, "*She* left in a hurry," nodding toward Zannie's exit.

"That poor girl has had a rough year." Mrs. Davis looked back at the doors. "Her dad died a few years ago, and she's coming up on the anniversary of her stepmom's death. She and her sister had to move in with an uncle. They've both struggled with all the changes."

Not to mention, her sister is a criminal, I thought.

We snuck glances at each other, all of us pretending Mrs. Davis was sharing completely new information. But then something the librarian had said shook an idea lose in my head, and I grabbed March's case files and began shuffling through all the papers.

"Oh," Mrs. Davis said. "You actually have something in common with Zannie. She's also asked me to help her do a little research on Blood Eagle and Marty Cavalier."

I stared at the librarian, unsure what to think of this new clue. Was Zannie trying to understand what had upset Zoey and provoked her to a life of crime? Maybe

275

Zannie didn't even know that Marty had stolen Blood Eagle from her stepmom.

When we didn't respond, Mrs. Davis asked, "So . . . have you tracked down your villain yet?"

"Vandal," March corrected.

"Oh, yes," Mrs. Davis agreed. "Or, more precisely, graffitist. Graffiti plus artist."

The bell rang and everyone at our table stood to leave, except me.

"Just a second," I said.

Mrs. Davis waved good-bye and began a walk-through of the library, grabbing loose books on tables and chairs. When I found what I had been looking for, I scrambled to catch up with the team.

"This Sunday is the anniversary of Claudia's death," I said, waving the obituary at them.

We stopped at the library doors, everyone looking at me blankly.

"So?" March finally asked.

"So," I said as we stepped into the hallway. "That's the big date we were looking for—the day Zoey will bomb Phoenix Rising."

But even as I said it, I realized it didn't matter anymore. Once we gave Officer Rhodes the files, the case would officially be closed. Although, that didn't mean we couldn't make sure the police actually prevented the bombing. After all, we didn't need to tell them that we had hacked Phoenix Rising's network and could still monitor their security footage.

The library doors clanged shut behind us as I brainstormed one final mission.

CHAPTER FORTY-THREE

Baa-chan was vacuuming in the living room when I got home from school, and she waved to me as I dropped my backpack in the entryway.

"Where's Mom?" I asked.

She turned off the vacuum cleaner. "She's in bed."

"What?" A chill blossomed in my chest and spread through my arms. "But I thought she was better."

"She's *getting* better," Baa-chan said. "It'll take a while to completely heal, and she'll still have bad days."

"But you're leaving tomorrow." Baa-chan had been preparing all week for her return trip to Japan. "Maybe we're not ready to be alone."

Baa-chan smiled, and for the first time I noticed the

same sprinkle of freckles across her cheeks as mine. And as Mom's. "You'll be fine," she said. "I'm certain of it."

She wrapped up the hose and moved into the kitchen to reorganize a cabinet she had been complaining about since she had arrived.

I wandered over to O-jizō-sama, where a stick of incense still burned in the little holder. Propped again the statue's base was a fuzzy black-and-white ultrasound image. *Mei* was written on the picture with a silver Sharpie in Mom's handwriting, and next to it, two kanji, written in Baa-chan's: 芽生. I didn't know exactly what it meant, but I recognized the last character: *life and growth*.

Mom came to tuck me in that night, the first time in a long time, and I snuggled deeper under the covers as she sat on the edge of my bed.

"Kazu," she said. "I didn't mean to scare you this afternoon. Baa-chan told me you were worried."

I brought my arms from under the covers and laid them next to me, and Mom grabbed one of my hands in hers. Genki had begun his ritual of digging around in my loose bedding to make it pillowy and dog-shaped.

"Sweetie, I feel like I've been in a coma, and now I'm awake, but I'm still really groggy and also rusty at mothering. I'll probably take a few more breaks than usual."

I shrugged, wanting to tell it her it wasn't a big deal but not trusting myself to speak.

"You would've made the best big sister." Her voice cracked a bit, but she coughed instead.

"You were going to name her Mei?"

She nodded. "That's a great name, right?"

"It's a really good name," I agreed.

She leaned down to kiss my cheek. "Well. Good night." As she got up, she looked around my messy room, probably wondering if I had cleaned it at all since Baa-chan had arrived. I had, thank you very much.

Genki's tail beat against the bedspread. He was better at showing his feelings than anyone else in this family.

"Good night, Mom," I whispered as she walked out my door, turning back to smile before she closed it behind her.

CHAPTER FORTY-FOUR

Baa-chan's suitcase sat by the door. We all walked into the backyard, where Dad had moved O-jizō-sama into the flower bed. The statue stood serenely in the dark soil, surrounded by orange-and-purple pansies.

Baa-chan knelt in the grass before the statue, and Mom and I knelt next to her. Genki plopped down behind us.

"I started to make this as a blanket when your mom told me she was pregnant," Baa-chan said. "Now I give it to O-jizō-sama in honor of Mei-chan."

I watched closely as Baa-chan wrapped the scarf around O-jizō-sama's neck two times. It hung from his shoulders and pooled in the dirt. She murmured

something in Japanese, and while I couldn't really understand what she was saying, I felt a sense of calm expand
in my chest as I thought of my sister, Mei, who I had
never met but who was still a part of our family. When I
snuck a peek at Mom, I saw large tears rolling down her
cheeks. Two weeks ago, that sight would have scared me,
but now I understood Mom needed to grieve for something we all had lost.

She was attending her group meetings, where she
talked about my sister with other moms who had had
miscarriages. She was also taking medicine that would
help her manage the sad feelings a little better. Even so,
I knew she would still have afternoons where she stayed
in her room and rested. But like Baa-chan said about the
temperature scarf, she was having more yellow days than
blue now.

"We should probably head to the airport," Dad
said, and then he followed us back into the house to the
front door.

Mom and I sandwiched Baa-chan in a hug, and I
buried my face in her shoulder.

"Kazu-chan," she whispered in my ear. "You are a
great girl, and I will feel lonely without you."

"I have something for you," I said, and dashed to
the kitchen counter to grab the collage I had made
her in art club. Small enough to fit inside her suitcase,

my art project had pictures of everyone in our family surrounded by kanji she had taught me to write: *love, family, happiness, life,* and *growth.* Most of them were complicated characters that were probably hard to read, but she clutched the foam board to her chest and beamed at me with crinkly eyes.

"And for you," she said, "I left a matching temperature scarf on your bed, like Mei's."

"Arigatou, Baa-chan," I said, hugging her waist.

• • •

March's sister Maggie drove us to the police station that night, and we all walked single file through the front door to the desk, where an older officer looked us over. March heaved the case files onto the counter and said, "We need to talk to Officer Rhodes."

"Regarding what, may I ask?" He leaned toward us and smiled, like he was asking what we wanted for Christmas.

"The comic book criminal," Madeleine said, adjusting her posture so that she stood straight and tall.

"The what?" The man wrinkled his nose at us.

"The vandal." March opened the folder and took out a handful of Madeleine's photographs, fanning them onto the counter.

The officer nodded before picking up the phone, pushing some buttons, and saying, "There are some kids here to see you about all that graffiti."

He watched us until Officer Rhodes pushed through a door behind the counter. "Ahh," he said, crossing his arms over his chest. "The Mystery Squad."

I narrowed my eyes, trying to be offended, but the more I repeated that title in my mind—Mystery Squad—the more I liked it.

"We're giving you our case files," March said, returning the photographs to the folder and pushing the thick bundle toward him. "With the most recent hit, we believe the vandal is going to bomb Phoenix Rising tomorrow. You need to stop her."

"Stop *her*?" he asked.

"It's a really long story." CindeeRae projected her voice into the small office, which had surprisingly good acoustics. "But the vandal is Claudia Reed's stepdaughter Zoey."

"Okay, I'll bite," he said, taking a step closer. "Who is Claudia Reed?"

"She's the artist who created the original Blood Eagle character," I said. "Marty Cavalier, the founder of Phoenix Rising, stole the idea, and Blood Eagle went on to become super famous, and Marty never gave Claudia any credit. Her stepdaughter found out and has been trying to tell the world through her graffiti."

Officer Rhodes stepped up to the counter and opened the folder, thumbing through all the information we had gathered. "This definitely sounds like an origin story worthy of a comic book vandal."

March and Madeleine both raised their eyebrows.

"What?!" Officer Rhodes said. "You didn't think I knew anything about comic books? I grew up on them."

"So you'll stop Zoey from bombing Phoenix Rising tomorrow?" CindeeRae asked.

"Now hold on," Officer Rhodes said. "What makes you so sure she's bombing Phoenix Rising tomorrow?"

We all looked at him. Was he joking? "Didn't you see her last hit?" I asked. "The phoenix in a cage. With a bomb?"

"And the anniversary of Claudia's death is tomorrow," March said. "Zoey wants to make sure Marty pays for what he did to her stepmom."

"All right, all right." Officer Rhodes held up his hands in surrender. "I'll definitely have my team take a look at all your work."

When we didn't leave, the older officer peeked around Officer Rhodes. "Do you kids need to call for a ride?"

"No," March said. "My sister's waiting for us."

As we turned to leave, Officer Rhodes said, "I do appreciate you turning this information over to us." He nodded, a real smile on his face. "Because we hate to think of you kids putting yourselves in danger. That's *our* job."

We all shuffled toward the door. Maybe Officer Rhodes didn't hate us after all, I thought. But still, as we left the police station, I saw him turn back to his office, abandoning our case files on the counter where we had left them.

CHAPTER FORTY-FIVE

The team lay on the floor of March's tree house, snuggled in sleeping bags and watching the Christmas lights flicker on the ceiling. Wedged between Madeleine and March, I told the last of the knock-knock jokes I knew.

"Harry up and answer the door!" I snorted at my punch line, even though it wasn't really funny. CindeeRae booed.

March's iPad was propped on the top of an upside-down bucket, still hacked into Phoenix Rising's security system. The device trilled with an alarm March had programmed to alert us each time the surveillance camera caught something. The video window flashed to life, and we all bolted upright as a cat sauntered across the screen.

"Stupid motion detector!" March said.

Even though we had closed the case, we had decided to have a sleepover at March's house, where we still might be able to watch the police wrap things up in real time. While we hoped Officer Rhodes had already talked to Zoey, we still weren't confident he had taken our evidence seriously.

Midnight would mark the official, one-year anniversary of Claudia Reed's death, the time we thought Zoey was most likely to bomb Phoenix Rising. We had already stuffed ourselves sick with cheeseballs, gummy sours, and pizza bites, and my eyelids were heavy. We had shared all the jokes, gossip, and ghost stories we knew, and my brain felt fuzzy. But in twenty minutes, it would officially be the one-year anniversary of Claudia's death, and I wanted to be awake for it.

• • •

I awoke to a high-pitched squeal, which I soon realized was the iPad alarm combined with March's shrieking. The tree house clock glowed 3:33, and I rolled out of my sleeping bag to see what the commotion was about. Madeleine rubbed her eyes while CindeeRae slept on, oblivious to the commotion. Was she wearing earplugs?

I knelt next to March in front of the iPad, the video screen staticky.

"What is going on?" I whisper-yelled.

"Zoey broke into Phoenix Rising!" He didn't even try to keep his voice down as he turned off the alarm. "WHY IS SHE BREAKING INTO PHOENIX RISING? WHERE ARE THE POLICE?"

Where *were* the police? And then I remembered Officer Rhodes leaving our case files on the counter at the police station. "The police aren't there because Officer Rhodes didn't believe us!"

Madeleine had finally untangled herself from her sleeping bag, and she stood behind us, hunched over so she wouldn't hit her head on the ceiling. "What's going on?"

"I'll tell you what's going on," I muttered, looking around the tree house for my shoes. "We have to do everything ourselves."

"What does that mean?" Madeleine asked.

"We've got to go to Phoenix Rising and stop Zoey from setting off a bomb," I said.

"And how are we going to do that?" March asked.

I stopped spinning around the tree house. We didn't have time to ride our bikes over, and going out on our own this late would definitely break some serious rules. We would need an adult to help.

CindeeRae had finally awoken to ask, sleepily, "Shouldn't we call the police?"

"No," I said, finding my shoes under an overturned bucket and dropping to the floor to put them on. "We'll get my mom."

• • •

"What are you talking about?" Mom's words slurred as she tried to wake up. March, CindeeRae, and Madeleine cowered out of sight at the top of the stairs. The four of us had ridden through the night to my house, where I had let us in with the hidden house key.

Dad sat up and peered at his phone. "Do you realize it's after midnight?"

"Yes!" I said, wanting my parents to fast-forward to being awake and agreeable. "And we have to hurry, or we'll be too late."

"Late for what?" Mom asked, still lying on her side, propped up on one elbow.

"I don't have time to explain," I said. "Except that we know who the vandal is, and we need to stop her." If I told them about the bomb, they'd never agree to help us. When they didn't move, I raised my voice and snapped, "Like now!"

"Calm down." Dad opened his phone. "If that's true, we should call the police."

"We already told them," I said. "And they didn't believe us."

Mom stood, wrapping her robe around herself and cinching it at the waist. "Maybe they'll believe an adult this time."

"Please, don't call the police." I stared at Mom, willing her to understand what I was trying to say. "She's only sixteen, and her stepmom died last year. Her dad died a few years before that, and she's sad. She's not acting like herself." I paused, trying to read Mom's face, still pinched with doubt. "It's like she's in a coma," I tried again, "only instead of hiding away, she's doing some bad things that could ruin her life."

Mom slid on her slippers and began to walk from the room, Genki padding after her. She startled at the top of the stairs, finally seeing the rest of the team. "Goodness," she said, clutching at her heart. "You scared me!"

"Sorry, Ms. J," March said, and then ducked his head into my parents' room. "Good evening, Mr. J."

"What the . . ." Dad muttered.

"Sorry," I said. "I couldn't just leave everyone at March's house."

Mom looked over her shoulder at me. "Well?" she asked. "Are you coming?"

"Yes!" I said, rushing after her.

CHAPTER FORTY-SIX

March, CindeeRae, and Madeleine squished together in the backseat of the car, while I sat up front with Mom. We drove in silence for one block before Mom said, "Okay. Spill it."

March and I took turns telling her the story, starting with the Super Pickle. She gasped when we told her that we had caught the vandal painting another mural on Hero Brigade, and then again when we described how someone dressed as Dark Writer had stolen the same comics we had attended ComiCanon to study for clues. And she nodded her understanding when we finally revealed that the mastermind behind this whole operation had actually been Claudia Reed's older stepdaughter, Zoey.

The silence grew as Mom drew closer to Phoenix Rising. The heater whooshed air into the car while Mom's nails clicked on the steering wheel.

When she finally spoke, her voice was loud. "So our goal is to stop Zoey from painting another mural on Phoenix Rising?"

"Well," CindeeRae said from the backseat. "Something like that."

Mom pulled into the parking lot, taking up two spaces in front. "What does she mean by that?" Mom asked.

March looked up from the iPad and whispered, "Zoey went in through the back—on the loading dock."

"And she hasn't come out yet?" I asked.

March waited for his iPad to connect to the store's Wi-Fi before flashing the staticky video screen at us as if that were an answer. "I don't think so."

"Wait a minute." Mom turned to me, glaring. "She broke into the building?"

"Yes?" I said, leaning away from her. "But if we can stop Zoey before she does anything bad, she won't get in as much trouble."

Mom cut her eyes at me, and I could tell she was thinking about what to do next. Finally, she got out of the car and shut the door so quietly the only noise it made was a small click. I followed her, but when my door wouldn't shut, I bumped it lightly with my hip.

Click. CindeeRae and Madeleine tumbled from the back, followed by March, who, still hypnotized by his iPad screen, slid from the backseat and slammed the door behind him, not looking up as he walked toward the building.

"Shhhhh," the four of us hissed at him.

March stopped and looked back at us, eyes wide. "What?"

I scoffed and led our group around the building to the back alley, where the door to the loading dock had been rolled open a couple feet, a skateboard propped up in the corner waiting for Zoey's return. As I climbed onto the dock, Mom grabbed my ankle. "No way," she whispered, tugging me back down.

"We have to confront her."

"We wait here." Mom folded her arms across her chest like parent armor. There was no getting through. "She left it open because she's coming back out this way."

"That's a good plan," March's voice croaked, and CindeeRae nodded her agreement.

Mom grabbed the skateboard and held it to her chest, sending the back wheels rolling in the night air. Then we pressed ourselves tight against the wall so Zoey wouldn't see our feet when she came out.

Our breathing staggered as we waited. March continued to watch his iPad screen, as if that view was better than the real one we had now.

We almost didn't hear her when she slid out, her body clearing the door and then stopping to drag her backpack behind her. It was only when she realized that her skateboard was gone that she spun around and found us watching her.

"What?" It came out in a squeak. Without waiting for an answer, she sprinted toward the other end of the alley.

"Zoey Carson," March called after her, and the girl slowed to a stop, her back still to us. "We know who you are, and if you leave now, we'll call the police."

Zoey turned slowly until she faced us, her bandanna covering the bottom half of her face. "And if I don't leave, what? We'll go out for breakfast? Become buddies?"

"We know you left a bomb," March said in a rush. "You need to destroy it. Now."

"What?!" Mom shrieked, and it echoed against the building.

"There may or may not be a bomb in the building," I whispered. I could see the muscles in Mom's jaw clench as her lips drew into a thin line.

Zoey took a few steps toward us, holding up what looked like a TV remote but was probably a detonator, with a button to set off the bomb. "And if I don't?" Her voice sounded so young.

March took one large step forward toward Zoey. Mom blocked him, moving to stand in front of the entire team.

I peeked around her and said, "You'll go to jail for a long time." Like, duh. Zoey was caught. I always wondered why criminals resisted arrest when they were so clearly trapped. Although she did have a bomb, and if it blew while we were standing here, it wouldn't be good for any of us.

"Put that down," Mom said, nodding at Zoey's hand.

Zoey looked at Mom, sizing her up. Mom wasn't very imposing in her cotton robe, but her mom-glare was still scary.

"I can tell you're sad," Mom said. "You've been sad for so long, it became easier to be angry."

Zoey laughed, and it echoed in the alley. "What do *you* know?"

"We know a lot," March said. "Your stepmom was a great comic book artist, and Marty cheated her so that she never got credit for Blood Eagle. You want people to know how amazing she was, especially since she's gone now." I looked at March, surprised.

She dropped her hands to her side, like March's words had zapped her strength. "All she'd ever done was take care of us." Zoey's voice was low, and I could hardly hear what she'd said. "Even though she's gone, I wanted to pay her back somehow."

"She wouldn't want this," Mom said.

We stood for a few seconds looking at each other, a cat meowing in the distance.

"So, what?" she asked. "I get the bomb and you let me go?"

I felt March tense beside me. He may have felt for Zoey's stepmom, but she had hurt his uncle Owen and the Super Pickle, and she'd have to pay for that.

I stepped away from Mom, closing the gap between us. "You get the bomb, turn yourself in, and we won't say anything about it."

"Why would I turn myself in?"

"Because you did some bad things," I said. "To people who never hurt you or Claudia. You have to make up for that."

"No way," she snapped, and began backing up. "It's not fair! He took everything."

"It's not fair," Mom said, shaking her head.

Zoey looked like she was deflating.

"We know who you are, sweetie," Mom said in her best and softest mom-voice. "Let us help you. It won't be as bad if you turn yourself in."

"You actually *don't* know who I am." Zoey pulled the bandanna from her face. Even in the dark night, barely catching the glow of a streetlamp, I could tell who she was.

"Zannie," I said. Zoey wasn't the vandal after all! Zannie Carson had painted all those murals by herself. She had masterminded the whole thing.

"And it's not, like, an exploding bomb, you know," she

said, waving the remote at us. "Just a smoke bomb, to ruin all the comics."

"You can't ruin the comics!" In the dark, March's pale face shone like the moon.

Zannie set the remote on the ground and began to back away again when Madeleine swooped from behind to slide-tackle her, soccer-style. Zannie tumbled into a heap, her backpack padding her fall. Somehow no one had noticed Madeleine sneaking down the backside of the alley to block Zannie's escape.

"Was that really necessary?" CindeeRae asked. I shushed her.

"Come on, Zannie." Mom re-cinched her robe tie. "Let's go get that smoke bomb."

CHAPTER FORTY-SEVEN

After a silent car ride to the police station, we walked Zannie up the front steps and dropped her at the same counter we had dropped our case files just yesterday. The same old officer from before looked us over and asked, "You again? What do you need this time?"

I nodded at Zannie, who looked at Mom before answering, "I want to turn myself in. I'm the graffitist."

I smiled to hear her use Mrs. Davis's descriptor.

"Vandal," March corrected.

The officer looked at her long and hard before letting out a chuckle. "Riiiiight."

A flare of anger burned my chest. "Why? 'Cause she's a kid? Or because she's a girl?!"

Mom tsked in warning, and the officer looked from me to her and then back to Zannie. "Oh," he said. "You're not kidding."

The officer had us wait on the bench by the door while he disappeared into the back room. Mom looked exhausted, ready to skulk back into her bedroom for a few more days. But she looked at Madeleine and asked, "Isn't your mother a lawyer?"

Madeleine nodded. Mom stood and pulled her phone from her robe pocket, stepping outside the door for privacy.

After she left, March beamed at us. "That was some great teamwork. I mean, it was shaky at first, but we really came together in the end."

I thought back to our work on the entire case, the miscommunications, the team operations, the secret missions, and the death-defying attempts to gather clues.

"*You* were horrible at first." CindeeRae nodded in agreement. "But *you* totally came together at the end."

"And where were you this whole time?!" Madeleine shrieked.

The policeman returned to his place behind the desk and shot us a warning glance. We all sank down in our seats.

"Preventing you guys from killing each other,"

CindeeRae whispered. "And I'm great at teamwork. A natural."

I thought back to all the times she'd tried to mend disagreements and safeguard our feelings. She wasn't wrong.

I whispered, "I just can't believe we didn't know it was Zannie from the very beginning."

Zannie had been watching us talk, her eyebrows high. "I'm right here, you know."

I looked at March. "What do you call a kid who's a genius at something? Like pro-level amazing?"

"A prodigy?"

"Yes!" I said, turning to Zannie. "You're a prodigy! Like a master artist—don't mess that up."

Before she could answer, Mom walked back in and sat down again, pulling me against her side, under the warmth of her arm.

Madeleine's mom, Zannie's uncle, and Officer Rhodes all arrived at the police station around the same time. Officer Rhodes studied our team before saying, "She really did try to bomb the place?"

"Not exactly," I said. "But she is ready to turn herself in."

March muttered, "We told you so."

Officer Rhodes stared March down, fiddling with the handcuffs on his belt. Then he called another officer to show Madeleine's mom, Zannie, and her uncle into a back room while he stayed to see us off. "You know the drill," he said. "Come back in for a statement tomorrow."

Even Mom looked too tired to turn this into a teaching moment. "Let's go home," she said, ruffling March's hair as she led us from the police station, her arms spread protectively around all of us.

CHAPTER FORTY-EIGHT

For the first time, the team got to watch Zannie begin one of her amazing murals, only she had permission to paint this one. Zannie had outlined a ginormous picture on the brick wall at Comic Warehouse that began with her stepmother sitting at a drafting table in the far corner, a scene from Blood Eagle erupting across the rest of the wall as if it had sprung to life from the page she drew.

March stood on a ladder painstakingly filling in the Blood Eagle's blue-black wings with a can of Zannie's special Montana spray paint. "Claudia bought me cases of this stuff after I first told her I wanted to be a street artist," she had said, her eyes shining as she stared into the sky. "She was so happy I wanted to be an artist, and even finished the inside of the garage so I could paint whatever I wanted on the walls."

Zannie's long, dark hair hung in a thick braid down her back as she checked on our progress. "Don't be so sloppy with that roller, CR," she yelled at CindeeRae, Madeleine's nickname for her already sticking. CindeeRae was in charge of the sky, which had to be rolled on since it required the most paint.

"I'm not sloppy," she called back, stepping over huge droplets of cornflower blue that spotted the gray tarp.

Zannie had sprayed each section of the mural with a small dot of paint and had assigned us each a color. I was in charge of the gold accents in the Blood Eagle's costume; Zannie said I had a knack. Madeleine documented the project with her phone's camera—pictures we hoped Zannie might be able to include in her application for the Denver School of the Arts.

Zannie had confessed to all the damage she had done as Dark Writer, and as a result she was ordered to pay a huge fine and perform one hundred hours of community service. March's mom, Candy, hired Zannie to work as an intern for her graphic design firm, and Zannie was using that money to pay off her debt. Meanwhile, she had offered to paint Comic Warehouse in preparation for a grand reopening that would celebrate Miguel, Owen, and Nia's new partnership as joint owners of the comic book store. The three were inside now, rearranging display cases to make room for Owen and Nia's inventory, and every now and then one of them would slip out to check our progress. Since Owen's online sales had exploded, he was considering quitting his day job to focus on this new venture. We'd be celebrating their partnership that Sunday with a new Defender campaign with Nia as Game Master.

The *Denver Chronicle* did a full-page article about the case, where Zannie, who went unnamed because she was still a kid, was able to tell her story. She took full responsibility for the damage she had caused, while also sharing pride for her stepmom's role as creator of Blood Eagle.

And with the news out about Blood Eagle, Marty Cavalier had agreed that Phoenix Rising would publish a commemorative set that included an introduction to Blood Eagle artist and creator, Claudia Reed. After working out all the legal issues for Zannie, Madeleine's mom had gotten Marty to agree to credit Claudia in all future Blood Eagle issues and reprints and pay for her contribution to the comic. That money would go into a trust fund for Zoey and Zannie.

Meanwhile, March, CindeeRae, Madeleine, and I were trying to come up with a name for our very successful detecting team. We had solved our second case without meddling—*too* much meddling, that is. While Officer Rhodes had been mostly pleased with the "research" we had done, he had still given us a stern lecture about avoiding danger and staying out of trouble.

"How about Sleuth Central?" I asked.

Zannie dipped one eyebrow down at me from where she stood painting details on her stepmom's face. "What are you talking about?"

March jumped in before I could answer. "We need a name for our detective team."

"Ohhhhhh," she said. "You mean like Mystery Incorporated?"

"Exactly!" I answered, happy that Zannie knew the official name of the Scooby team.

"Okay." Zannie nodded thoughtfully. "Super Snoopers."

"Hmmm." I didn't love it.

Madeleine laughed. "That's pretty spot-on." She held her phone up to take a picture of me, and I flashed a peace sign. "But I also like Elementary Detectives. You know, 'cause we're in elementary school?"

"Case Nuts," CindeeRae chirped.

"Clues-R-Us," March added.

Zannie chuckled while March, CindeeRae, and Madeleine groaned.

"I know!" I yelled, thinking back to the night we had given Officer Rhodes our case files. "The Mystery Squad."

"Not bad," March said while CindeeRae nodded.

"I like it," Madeleine agreed, holding up her camera to catch us all in a selfie.

We chatted and laughed as we worked on Zannie's mural, the sky turning purple on the horizon while the smell of spray paint drifted toward the clouds.

I guess it didn't really matter what we called ourselves, as long as *we* knew we were a team.

Author's Note

When they were little, my three kids gravitated to all things geeky. Comic books, superhero movies, cult cartoons, obscure anime, cosplay. You name it, they loved it.

At first their interests puzzled me, until I remembered that at six years old my Wonder Woman obsession had evolved into a bone-deep belief that the superhero had given me up for adoption so that she could solve crimes.

It was possible my children had gotten The Geek from me.

Even as a single mom, I did my best to enable my three kids to follow the fandoms of their hearts. This meant that, between my two boys, I would make over seven Spider-Man birthday cakes. I would enlist the help of family and friends in tracking down the rarest My Little Pony figurines as gifts for my daughter. And I may or may not have shaved my eldest bald so that he could realistically portray Aang, the Last Airbender, the Halloween of his seventh year.

I barely blinked when my future husband told me he had hundreds of comic books in his collection, enough board games to start his own store, and a catalog of nerdy knowledge I couldn't begin to fathom.

Not only was he perfect for me; he was perfect for my children.

Those early years we cobbled together a seven-kid-big blended family that relied heavily on all The Geek we held in common. So it's not surprising that this book is a celebration of those geekdoms we love. I'm grateful to creators who build worlds our little fankids have enjoyed for nearly a decade now and will probably continue to love and share for decades to come. I hope *Kazu Jones and the Comic Book Criminal* represents just how meaningful those stories can be.

Acknowledgments

It definitely takes a village to build a book. There are so many people who have accompanied me on this journey, and I'll be continually grateful to everyone mentioned in the first book's acknowledgments!

The second book has garnered its own support group, and I want to thank everyone involved in its creation. I wouldn't be here without the encouragement and support of my agent, Carrie Pestritto.

Thanks to the whole Disney family, but especially Laura Schreiber for believing in this story, and to Hannah Allaman, my soul editor, who endured a very messy draft to help me bring out this story's happy heart. The amazing cover was designed by Joann Hill and Jamie Alloy and illustrated by Grace Hwang.

To my early readers for giving me feedback in the midst of the holidays, I still owe you! They include my best writing friend, Bridget Baker, and critique partners extraordinaire Megan Clements and Diana Tracy.

In this book, Kazu's grandma (Baa-chan) comes to stay with the family and introduces some Japanese cultural elements. Yumi Seavey and Mariko Brayley, thank you so much for reading through the first draft to see if those elements rang true to your Japanese-American experience.

I'll be forever grateful to Misa Sugiura, a tremendous author herself, for performing a sensitivity read and helping me recognize additional cultural shortcomings in the more polished draft. I'm not delusional enough to believe my revisions resulted in perfect representation, but with Misa's thoughtful feedback, it came a lot closer. All remaining mistakes I readily accept as my own.

To my newest critique group, thank you for inviting me to join the Goldies at the perfect time! I've never experienced such a comfy fit! Megan Clements, Annie Bailey, and Jeigh Meredith! I foresee many, many books in our futures!

My parents and siblings have been a tremendous support, cheering for me and sharing my social media posts, and my sister Jen is now officially my hometown agent, scheduling school visits and signings for me. Seriously, it's a lot. Love you guys!

And of course, what would I do without my amazing family that endures both my ridiculously happy and meltdown author moments? You guys are the best fans a girl could have: Harrison (and his wife, Katlyn), Kaleb, Leah, Claire, Zack, Carma, and Greyson. And of course, my husband and creative partner, Mike Holyoak, who inspires and encourages me daily. Every writer should have a Mike. No, you can't have mine.

Finally, I'm so thankful to all the readers—honorary members of the Mystery Squad, who have followed Kazu to this second book. I hope you love this story even more than the first and share it with other readers like yourself!

Happy detecting and reading!